THE BEST OF BIGGLE

A SCIENCE FICTION SHORT STORY COLLECTION
OF THE BEST EARLY WORKS BY

LLOYD BIGGLE, JR.

EDITED BY

KENNETH LLOYD BIGGLE AND

DONNA BIGGLE EMERSON

WILDSIDE PRESS

Copyright © 2014 by Kenneth Lloyd Biggle
and Donna Biggle Emerson.
Published by Wildside Press LLC.
www.wildsidebooks.com

CONTENTS

EDITOR'S NOTE 7
BEACHHEAD IN UTOPIA 8
HORNET'S NEST 19
MATING INSTINCT 31
THE MADDER THEY COME 44
TRAVELING SALESMAN 55
ESIDARAP OT PIRT DNUOR 71
LESSON IN BIOLOGY 93
ON THE DOUBLE 102
THEY LIVE FOREVER 116
WHO STEALS MY MIND... 121
AN ALIEN BY ANY OTHER NAME 136

EDITOR'S NOTE

Dr. Lloyd Biggle, Jr., my father, died on September 12, 2002. He left behind enough unfinished story outlines and manuscripts for another complete lifetime of writing.

One of the last story collection ideas my father proposed to my sister and me was a set of early science fiction short stories he considered to be his favorites. He had the list of titles compiled. Some were in manuscript form and some were in science fiction magazines from the 1950's and 1960's. However, due to technology changes all had to be converted to electronic format. That meant actually sitting down and re-typing them. With the help of my sister, Donna Biggle Emerson, this has been accomplished and we are now able to present to you the author's choice of "best of".

Although these stories, with the exception of "Alien by Any Other Name," have been previously published, they can be difficult to locate due to their age. I am delighted to be able to share this collection of early stories by Lloyd Biggle, Jr. with you.

—Kenneth Lloyd Biggle, 2013

BEACHHEAD IN UTOPIA

First Publisned in *Omega*, 1973

Coming from the board room with a stack of papers, Miss Philp said plaintively, "It isn't enough that it's E-day and also the end of the month. *They* want the annual report released today."

Miss Rodney rippled a stack of data cards, fixed her myopic gaze on Miss Philp, and asked absently, "What was that? Oh. E-day and the end of the month aren't what snarls things up. It's the board meeting. As the members walk in they suddenly remember all the things they were supposed to do between meetings but didn't. Research is in turmoil."

Miss Philp sniffed. "Research goes into turmoil whenever anyone asks a question. They think they're being imposed on if they're asked to work one day a month." She seated herself at the voicewriter, donned the microphone, and said grumpily, "I'll be dictating all day. The board'll revise every page six times."

Mr. Helpflin, of the Records Section, looked in at them, nodded, asked, "Has Mr. Dorr been here?"

"He's at the meeting," Miss Philp said.

"I didn't know they'd started. Is there any way to get a message to him?"

Miss Philp smiled coyly. "There might be—if it's important enough."

"Fellow downstairs wants an interview."

Miss Philp sniffed. "Is it about an extension?"

"Well—yes."

"He's on today's list, too, I suppose."

"Tell him every case is reviewed by the full board before finalizing."

"In my opinion, the fellow deserves some consideration. Is there any chance that Mr. Dorr would see him?"

"No chance at all," Miss Philp said firmly.

"Do you have his name and number?" Miss Rodney asked.

Helpflin glanced at a slip of paper. "William Zarny. F-97-043-15."

"I'll look him up. If Mr. Dorr happens to wander through here, I'll tell him the case interests you, and I'm sure he'll see that the board takes a careful look at it. I won't promise anything, though. Usually Mr. Dorr stays in the room until the meeting is over, and if anyone interrupts a board meeting, it'd better be important. I mean *really* important."

"This is *really* important—to William Zarny," Helpflin said grimly.

"If *you* want to take the chance—"

"No, thank you. If you see Mr. Dorr, please tell him about it."

He left with a nod and a smile, and Miss Philp sniffed again and loaded the voicewriter's feed hamper with masters and duplicating sheets. Miss Rodney was flipping through a stack of files, and when she found the one she wanted she opened it and drawled, 'Well wouldn't you know!"

"Know what?" Miss Philp asked.

"William Zarny. He had the full two years of training, and he didn't do a lick of work for the next two years plus three extensions."

"That's what I figured. I mean, I thought the F list had been liquidated. Three extensions are as many as the law allows, isn't it?"

Miss Rodney nodded. "I'll tell you this much—I certainly wouldn't mention *this* case to Mr. Dorr. Zarny's one of those slobs who figures society'll support him in grand style for the rest of his life, and suddenly it's E-day and he's used up his extensions. An interview with Mr. Dorr—indeed!"

She hunched her shoulders resignedly and began matching data cards with files. Miss Philp threw a switch, took a deep breath, and began to dictate. "*International Poverty Control Agency, United States Branch. Tenth Annual Report. It is with understandable pleasure that your National Poverty Control Board announces new and dramatic progress toward a goal that seemed unattainable only a decade ago: the total elimination of poverty from our midst. Occasional setbacks, such as the failure of a major industry during the past year, have been taken in stride. . . .*"

Her voice droned on, expertly inflicting the chirps and grunts to which the machine's punctuation marks were attuned.

William Zarny entered the first bar he came to and ordered a drink. The bartender took his credit card, glanced at it, glanced again, slid it into the register, and touched a button. He returned with the drink, remarking, "Expires today."

Zarny nodded. He downed the drink with one gulp and marched away.

At the Christian Unity Center he entered the Protestant offices. The receptionist smiled at him. "Back again?"

"They said I might see Bishop Corlett today."

"Zarny, isn't it?"

She flipped a switch. Do you have a William Zarny on Bishop Corlett's list?"

The flat answer came a moment later. "No."

"Whom did you talk with?" The receptionist asked.

"Mrs. Warren."

She flipped another switch. "Mrs. Warren, there's a William Zarny here. He says you told him—"

"I couldn't work him in," Mrs. Warren answered. "Tell him to come back tomorrow.

"Today is my E-day," Zarny said desperately.

"Today is his E-day," the receptionist said. "He's been coming here for months. Isn't there someone—"

"Send him up. I'll see."

Mrs. Warren indicated an interview room, and after a tedious half-hour wait an owlish-looking young man walked in, nodded, took the seat across from him. "I'm the Reverend Walter Kammity. Something I can do for you?"

"I hoped someone here might be able to find me a job."

The Reverend stroked a smooth cheek thoughtfully. "There are four governmental agencies and I don't know how many private ones—"

"I've tried *everywhere*."

"I see. Well, Mrs. Warren will give you a card to fill out, and—"

"I filled one months ago. And today is my E-day."

"I see. Why did you wait until the last minute?"

"I've been trying to see Bishop Corlett for months."

"We aren't exactly in the employment business," the Reverend said reproachfully. "And the Bishop is a very busy man."

"I'll do *anything*."

"That's what they all say—on E-day. You should have been willing to do anything a year ago."

"I was. I've done nothing but look for a job for almost three years. They gave me special training, you see, and then . . ."

"Then they couldn't find a job for you. Most unfortunate, but those things happen."

"Anything at all . . ."

The Reverend shook his head. "The law is the law, you know. Sometimes the welfare of society requires measures that impose sacrifices on individuals. I'm sure that none of us would want to return to the old system, where poverty bred crime and more poverty, and children grew up in an environment of material and spiritual degradation and extracted revenge by preying on their fellow men for the remainder of their lives. By keeping the welfare lists at a minimum we're able to give an unemployed worker's family a respectable standard of living and maintain that until he's had ample time to find employment, but even in these prosperous times we can't support indigent families indefinitely on that basis. If we didn't establish a cutoff date and enforce it, in a very short time the old tragic cycle would be operating again."

"I don't care about myself," Zarny said desperately. "But my kids are bright, and if they have half a chance . . ."

"You've had two years of training, you say, and then two more years plus whatever extensions you were allowed. That adds up to almost five years, which was surely ample time in which to give them a chance. Have you told them?"

"No. I didn't want to . . ."

"Did you send them to school today?"

Zarny nodded.

"It's best that way," the Reverend said approvingly. "There's no point in worrying the little ones about something that's beyond their control. I've seen some utterly shameful scenes result when the parents thoughtlessly told their children. Well. All I can do is express my regret and assure you that, compared with the old system, this is much, much the better solution." He fumbled in a pocket and laid a token on the table. "I'd suggest that you stop in the chapel on your way out. This will give you two free prayers in the Meditation Alcove—wait. You still have your credit card, don't you? Then you won't need this." He pocketed the toke and opened a memo book. "William Zarny. Wife's name? Children and ages? He scribbled the information. "I'll include you in my devotions tomorrow. No charge for that, of course. Good Morning."

The receptionist glanced at Zarny's face and said, "I'm sorry."

"Thank you for trying," Zarny said.

"I wonder—I've heard that Father Wilks has had some success at finding jobs. Just a moment." She telephoned, asked a question, and thoughtfully replaced the receiver. "He does find one now and the, but he has a waiting list of his own parishioners."

Zarny nodded and said with a wistful smile, "Thank you. I probably won't see you again."

He headed up the street toward the Municipal Employment Office. He'd been there every working day for more than two years and he knew that he didn't stand a chance, but he wasn't ready to face his wife and children. Not yet. Not until he had to.

Mr. Helpflin met Mr. Dorr in the corridor and asked, "Did Miss Rodney speak to you, sir?"

"About what?" Dorr asked.

Helpflin consulted his slip of paper. "William Zarny. F-97-043-15. He's on today's E-list."

"What about him?"

"It's rather complicated. Somebody made a colossal goof, and he's paying for it."

"What sort of goof?"

"Well—he was an expert computer technician. The old General Data Corporation's M1095. It's obsolete now, sir, and as fast as it was replaced with the advanced models the 1095 technicians found themselves out of work."

"Happens all the time," Dorr said cheerfully. "Why didn't Zarny train on one of the advanced models?"

"He did, sir. That is, he thought he did, but when he finished he couldn't find employment. He's been trying, really working at trying, but—nothing. I first heard about it this morning, and it sounded fishy to me."

"I should say so. Computer technician is a demand occupation."

"So I checked his record. His two years of training were put in on the 1108—which was obsolete before he finished. No wonder he couldn't find work!"

"I see," Dorr said thoughtfully.

"And he isn't eligible for another training course until he's worked for five years."

"It was the Training Center's goof," Dorr said. "Let *them* straighten it out. They can waive the five-year requirement for cause, and their own goof should be cause enough. Get in touch with them now, and if they'll accept him for more training, we can grant him an extension."

"He's already had the maximum."

"Well, we can waive that for cause, and his acceptance in a training program would be cause enough. The board has broad powers of discretion, you know. It doesn't use them impulsively, but it won't knowingly liquidate a man who's potentially useful. It'll be meetings the rest of the afternoon. If you can work something out with the Training Center, get word to me right away."

William Zarny left the fourth employment office. He'd skipped lunch; he hadn't felt like eating. He had two choices left—to go home and wait, or to go down fighting. He chose to fight. He went to a car rental agency, where the clerk looked at his credit card suspiciously and remarked, "Expires at five o'clock. Got a renewal?"

Zarny shook his head.

"E-day, eh? You wouldn't be thinking of taking your family and skipping, would you?"

"How far could I go on an expired credit card?" Zarny asked bitterly.

"What do you want the car for?"

"To look for a job."

"Did you apply for an extension?"

"I've already had the maximum."

The clerk said thoughtfully, "just a moment." He called to the clerk at the next window, "Wynn, weren't you saying something about some unemployed guy who finagled ten extensions?"

"Sure, why do you ask?"

"This fellow has used up his extensions. How was it managed?"

"Special case," Wynn said. "Guy'd been disabled in an industrial accident. Something about his spine. The doctors were confused and kept thinking maybe he'd be able to work again. It was medical extensions that he got. Eventually the doctors decided he was a hopeless case, so—no more extensions. They took him and his family last E-day."

"This fellow's E-day is today. He wants a car to look for a job."

"A little late for that isn't it?" Wynn asked.

Zarny did not answer. He was tired of explaining about those two years and nine months of searching, and applying, and waiting in anterooms, and arguing with secretaries and receptionists, and filling out forms and data cards that would be filed and forgotten.

"Sorry," the clerk said. "I just can't take the risk. I don't want to lose my job. In this occupational class, one bad judgment mark and I'd be on my way to E-day myself."

"I understand," Zarny said. "Thanks."

He turned away, more resigned than resentful. It hadn't been a good idea anyway. He had little time left, and he shouldn't be wasting it driving around. Outside, his gaze focused on the massive, ugly tower of the Federal Building—which, and everyone knew, had more computers per unit of floor space than any other building in the city. He headed that way, walking quickly.

Miss Philp, grumbling that they meant to keep her there all night, began dictating page seven of the fourth time. She reached the bottom of a column of figures and paused for breath. Miss Rodney was sorting through the next group of files. A messenger entered and handed her an envelope, and she glanced at it skeptically. *Mr. Dorr—Urgent. Deliver immediately.* "I'll bet." She opened it. "William Zarny again!"

"What about him?" Miss Philp asked.

"Something about his classification. It can't be all *that* urgent, but it's not my neck. Helpflin signed it. Still, just to be on the safe side—why don't you take it in when you have the next pages read?"

The receptionist said firmly, "I don't have to check. We haven't had a call for that job code for years."

"Please check anyway," Zarny said.

She shrugged. "If you insist. But I know—" She broke off as a light flashed. "Yes, Mr. Brakely?"

"Have you found anyone who can service a 1440?"

"No, sir. I've checked all the employment serviced, and—"

"Get on the phone and borrow a technician from someone. We're already a week behind with the tax statements, and the whole third floor is sitting around waiting on that dratted machine."

"I'll try, sir." She buzzed off.

Zarny swallowed and asked, "Is that a GDC1440?"

The receptionist nodded.

"That's my machine!"

"No." She shook her head emphatically. "Yours is the 1108."

"I should know. I had two years of training on the 1440!"

"Let's see your classification card again." She snapped it into a machine, read off the code, opened a classification manual. "'A' means you're a class-one technician, 'G' is for General Data Corporation, 'K' means the 1100 series machines, 'D'—"

Zarny stared at her. "I never knew that. I mean, they gave me the card, and I assumed— No wonder I couldn't get a job!"

"You actually trained on the 1440?"

Zarny nodded. "Trained on it for two years, and they've sent me their modification specifications ever since."

"Then someone punched your master card wrong," the receptionist said. She pressed a button. "Mr. Brakely? I have a man here—he had the wrong classification, but he claims that he trained on the 1440s."

"We'll soon find out," Brakely growled. "Send him up."

"Any reply yet?" Mr. Helpflin asked.

"The memo just went in," Miss Rodney said.

"But I marked it *urgent*!"

"So how urgent is urgent?" Miss Rodney asked.

Helpflin glanced at the clock. "Those who've had extensions are always processed first, and he's had three extensions. He'll be one of the first ones taken."

"So? It's only four o'clock."

"That leaves just an hour, and I don't know how long it takes to process a cancellation."

"What's all the fuss about?"

"This fellow trained on the latest-model computers, but someone made an error in coding his classification. His data card makes him an expert on an obsolete model, so of course no one would hire him. Now that his classification has been corrected, he can go to work anywhere. They tell me downstairs that two 1440 technicians are needed in the building and they'll hire him this afternoon if he'll apply." He glanced at the clock again. I'm going in there and straighten this out now."

"It's your funeral," Miss Rodney muttered, but Helpflin marched away. He was back again two minutes later, triumphantly waving an official cancellation card.

"Now all I have to do is find a messenger, and—no. I'm taking this over to E-quarters myself.

"A short circuit in bank ten," Zarny announced.

"How long will it take to fix it?" Brakely demanded.

"I've already fixed it."

"The devil! And you say you've been out of work—how long?"

"After I finished retraining, two years and nine months."

"Those idiots!" Brakely said disgustedly. "But why didn't you catch the error yourself?"

"You can't tell that a card is punched wrong just by looking at the holes," Zarny said. "Even if I'd put it in a machine, that particular code wouldn't have meant anything to me without a manual. And no one ever said, 'We don't need anyone for our 1108's.' They always said, 'We don't have any openings in your classification,' and naturally I assumed that they were referring to the 1440's"

"Everyone needs 1440 technicians," Brakely said. "I'm putting you on the night shift. See how many machines you can have operating by morning."

"Yes, sir. But this is my E-day, you see—"

"I understand. I'll take care of that. You concentrate on those 1440's."

Miss Rodney and Miss Philp, starting their second hour of non-compensated overtime because they could not leave until the board adjourned, had their boredom relieved momentarily by a clash between Mr. Helpflin and Mr. Dorr.

"We issued a cancellation," Dorr said. "I handed it to you myself. What'd you do with it?"

"I delivered it in person."

"So what was the trouble?"

"You didn't grant an extension. They crossed off his name, but the minute his time expired the master E-computer issued a warrant for him."

"I see. We didn't think about that—busy day, you know."

"That warrant overruled the cancellation. Without an extension it had no legal validity. Zarny's wife and children were picked up on schedule and taken directly to the ovens. In the meantime, the fellow got himself a job—"

"Really? Good for him."

"His employer sent the information and a request that he be removed from the E-list. Because he wasn't home when the E-squad came for his family, a warrant had been posted on him. He was eligible for E-treatment on sight because of the expiration. As soon as his boss's message hit the master computer, the computer dispatched a squad to pick him up at his place of employment. Imagine that—arresting a man on his job and hauling him away to be exterminated because he's unemployed."

"Did they get it straightened out?"

"Of course. The error in his classification has been corrected, and he's been removed from the E-list because he's now employed. But he and his family are still dead."

"So why did you call me out here? There's nothing *we* can do about it."

"I called you out to tell you that the board is going to have some explaining to do. The man's employer was the Federal Government, and the local office is suffering from an acute shortage of computer technicians. The office manager is threatening to demand a Congressional investigation."

"That's easily taken care of," Dorr said blandly. "Give him a priority and find the technicians he needs. Until you do, loan him one of ours." He turned to Miss Philp. "A few changes in this page, please. These are the last, I promise. We're down to our final order of business."

He hurried away. Helpflin stonily headed in the other direction. Miss Philp flipped a switch and donned the microphone. "*Because of the low unemployment rate and the anticipated continuing reductions in joblessness, this branch of the Poverty Control Agency will be able to cut its staff immediately by twenty percent. Further personnel reductions of at an additional thirty percent should be possible during the coming year, with a resultant savings—*"

Miss Rodney gasped, "What was that?"

Miss Philp looked up in surprise, turned off the voicewriter. "I wasn't paying attention. I could dictate in my sleep, and after a day like this I probably am. Cut its staff . . . further personnel reductions . . . *oh!*"

They stared at each other.

The board's final order of business.

Dismissal notices.

HORNET'S NEST

First published in *If Science Fiction*, September 1959

They sat in the captain's quarters, relaxed in the easy silence of close friendship as they absently sipped drinks and watched the monitor of the ship's scanner screen. There was Captain Miles Front, big, formidable-looking, a healthy and robust forty-five. There was Clyde Paulson, his brilliant young navigator. There was the expedition's chief scientist, Doctor John Walter, a pleasant-looking, balding man of indeterminate age.

It was Paulson who broke the silence. "I have an important mission of my own," he said.

They regarded him with amused skepticism, and he grinned good-naturedly.

"An ancestor of mine, my great-great-great—how many generations has it been now? Anyway, old Grandfather Paulson left Earth in some kind of disgrace. The details have been forgotten, down through the years, but the legend has been passed along as a family joke. I don't know whether he joined the colonists to run away, or whether that was someone's idea of a good way to get rid of him. Anyway, it's kind of a pledge to the family's honor that the first one to get back to Earth will check up and see whether Grandfather Paulson has been exonerated, or pardoned, or acquitted, or whatever. That's my mission. Not that it will make any difference to Grandfather Paulson one way or the other."

"So that's why you were so eager to make this trip," the captain said. "You needn't have bothered. A lot of chance you will have to rake up a scandal that old!"

"I thought it was a pretty good excuse," said Paulson.

Doctor Walter pointed at a boldly glimmering star. "You're sure that's the one?"

Paulson grinned, and Captain Front chuckled dryly.

"Disappointed to find it looks just like another star?" the captain said.

"Maybe," Walter said dreamily. "This is a different kind of mission for me. It's a pilgrimage. There are maddening blank spaces in the information the colonists brought with them about this solar system. I hope to fill in some of those. I'd like to fill all of them in."

"You may be able to," the captain said. "Remember that Earth's scientists haven't been standing still all this time. They must have progressed beyond the point they'd reached when the colonists left. Perhaps they'll have everything you want waiting for you."

Walter shrugged and the captain chuckled again, and said to Paulson, "I've disappointed him. He doesn't want to find the answers on file. He wants to dig them out for himself."

Doctor Walter said to the captain, "What's your mission?"

"To get us there and back. And frankly—" he turned to look at the lone, flickering star—"there are angles to this thing that bother me. It's just possible that our mother planet might not be at all glad to see us."

"It should greet us with open arms," Walter said. "The population problem was serious when the colonists left. It will be critical by now. We can use the people, and Earth should be able to spare as many as we want. Our science is bound to be ahead of Earth's in many respects, and we know they can't match our starships, or we would have heard from them before now. Ships that bring out new colonists can take essential raw materials back to Earth. Cooperation will benefit all of us."

"It should," the captain said, "But we don't know how Earth will look at it. When the original colonists left, there was supposed to be a new ship every couple of years. Nothing has been heard from Earth since. It looks as if Earth simply wrote us off and forgot about us. Now that we've built our own civilization, and maybe done far better than Earth expected, we might not be welcomed back. Earth might be jealous. Or it might have a guilty conscience. It *should* have."

"Faulty navigation," Paulson suggested.

"An occasional ship might go astray. Not all of them. No. The thing has me worried. That's why I want to hit Pluto Base and planet-hop our way in. Give Earth notice that we're coming, and a chance to get used to the idea before we arrive."

Doctor Walter brightened. "Pluto Base. I wonder if they ever found a tenth planet."

Clyde Paulson laid out a perfect interception course for Pluto, and he was still grinning with satisfaction when they brought the ship down. The captain rotated the scanner and looked broodingly at the frigid, airless landscape.

"Is this Pluto Base or isn't it?" he growled.

"It is," Paulson said confidently.

"They're taking their time about sending out a reception committee. They should have picked us up hours ago. Some security system!"

They waited, straining their eyes to pick out details. Doctor Walter came into the control room. He glanced at the screen and exclaimed, "Why, there's nothing there!"

"Pluto Base is underground," the captain said, rotating the scanner again. "Or at least it was. I imagine it still is."

"Stop!" Paulson shouted. "Over there on that hill—wouldn't that be the base entrance?"

The captain threw in the magnification unit.

"It could be," Doctor Walter said.

"It is," the captain said. "And the airlock is open."

They landed, watched, saw nothing more and entered.

They went cautiously through the empty corridors. Equipment was there. Supplies were there. Machinery was in operating condition. All signs indicated a hasty departure.

"They left just before lunch," Doctor Walter said in the mess room. "The food is still here, laid out for them."

"All we'd have to do" Captain Front said, "is close the airlock, start the air machines and take over. The supplies would last us indefinitely. I can understand that they might find reasons to abandon this base, but why would they pull out and leave all this stuff?"

"The transmitters are in working condition," a communications officer said. "It'd be easy to start the power station. Shall we call Earth and ask them?"

The captain said, "Now that I think of it, we haven't picked up any signals from Earth, have we?"

There was an uneasy silence. The captain looked around at the faces that peered grotesquely at him through spacesuit faceplates.

"Then we won't call Earth," he said, "until we're certain just what might be there to answer us."

They spiraled slowly in toward the sun, probing, exploring, searching, constantly alert and cautious. They touched Neptune and Uranus and such moons as looked promising. They touched a half-dozen of the moons of Saturn. The bases, where they found them, were desolate and abandoned.

Not until they reached the moons of Jupiter did they find the first dusty remnants of human bodies.

"Whatever it was," Doctor Walter said, "it happened quickly."

"Attack?" the captain asked.

"I can't believe it. An attack can take people by surprise but they're not too surprised to know what's happening. Some of them would take defensive measures. Most of them would act for their own safety. These people were stricken down in the everyday routine of living."

"Disease? Plague?"

"It wouldn't strike everyone at the same instant. This did,"

"We might as well go on," the captain said. "If it's necessary, we can hit any of these places again on the way out."

* * * *

From that moment they all knew. No one talked about it. No one even hinted at the cold fear that twisted within him. The communications men continued to search vainly for signals. The scientists carried on their observations. The ship's officers rotated the scanner toward a far-off corner of emptiness and strained to see a fleck of light that would be Earth when they came closer. And they all knew what they would find there.

On Mars, it was no longer desolate bases. It was annihilated cities—except that stone and mortar and steel were untouched. The people had been struck down as unsuspectingly as if a remote deity had suddenly decided upon doomsday. The flimsy atmosphere domes had lost their air and the buildings stood in excellent preservation, a futile monument to a wasted dream.

And then there was Earth. Rolling green hills, majestic cities, awesome natural wonders, all familiar, like a long-forgotten love. Majestic cities of the dead. Towns and villages and hamlets and solitary dwelling of the dead.

They had known what they would find, and they found it, and still were stunned.

"It hit the whole solar system," Doctor Walter said, snapping his fingers, "just like that."

Paulson objected. "There weren't any bodies at the outer bases. Those people had a chance to get away—or at least to try."

The captain nodded. "I have a hunch that Venus and Mercury were caught. If so, that means it struck the solar system out as far as Jupiter's moons. Something from the sun?"

Walter pondered the suggestions, and shook his head. "Heat would have left traces. So would any kind of radiation I know of that could do this. How long has it been? We should be able to pick up the exact date."

They landed at New Washington. The specialists, the experts, went grimly to work. The archeologist who had come to probe eagerly some faded secrets of Earth's ancient peoples found himself with the problem of an extinct interplanetary civilization. The botanist could only wonder at the survival of abundant flora when all fauna had perished. The bacteriologist, the chemist, the physicists, the military intelligence officer masquerading as a diplomat, all pondered the possible source of the catastrophe.

Clyde Paulson, unwanted by the scientists and unneeded by his ship, found his way into the military records section and gazed disheartened at the mountainous files of films.

"Well," he said, "since I've got nothing better to do..."

* * * *

He searched the index references, found Paulsons in quantity, but no mention of his dishonored ancestor.

"Odd," he said, "He couldn't have been such a scoundrel that they destroyed his records."

He prowled through the building, sampling the priceless military secrets of a lost civilization, getting himself lost, becoming more frustrated by the hour. He sat down to analyze his problem.

"Permanent records," he mused. "Those would be records that are complete. In other words, when a man's service was terminated, they filmed his records and put them in the permanent file. There would be another file for those on active service. Which means that old Grandfather Paulson was still considered on active service when it happened. Which is odd, because he left with the colonists. Could that mean the colonists..."

Impossible. A shipload of colonists wouldn't kill off the civilization that mothered it, and then leave for the stars in search of breathing room—even if it had the power.

He continued his search, and eventually he found active records of the military services. They were crudely kept files containing paper documents and records and even these were only abstracts of service records. He comprehended, at length, that the complete records were kept with the man at his point of service. What a prodigious amount of effort to devote to such a simple matter as record keeping!

"Paulson, Paul," the file said. "Space Navy. Serial Number 0329 B9472 A8974."

Paulson took the file and carried it out into the fresh air, to a plot of tangled grass where there were no bleached bones to dishearten him. He settled down to read of the bright development of a promising military career that had ended in disgrace.

Paul Paulson had held the rank of captain in the Space Navy. He was a pilot of the highest qualifications. He had served with distinction on a number of dangerous missions. His last assignment had been the Space Navy Base on Callisto, Jupiter Command. The record concluded with the notation of a court-martial on a charge of insubordination, and the terse verdict:

Guilty.

Accompanying the file was a smaller folder, labeled, "Summary of Court-Martial Proceedings Against Paul Paulson." The contents of the folder had been withdrawn for study, a notation informed him. He opened it and found a single sheet of paper that had been overlooked or unwanted.

* * * *

Paulson said to the captain, "Have they found anything?"

"They found one thing. This happened just about two Earth months after the colonists left Pluto Base. I remember something in the old records about their communications with Earth breaking down sooner than they'd expected. Now we know why. It looks as if the human race missed extermination by an eyelash. What have you been up to?"

"I found a personnel file on Grandfather Paulson. I suppose no one will object to my taking it."

"None of the natives I've met will object. Have you vindicated the old man?"

"He received a court-martial for insubordination. That would be no disgrace in our family. Funny thing, though –the trial summary is missing, except for one statement by Grandfather Paulson. Interested?"

"Let's have it."

Captain Front took the paper and read:

"To whom it may concern: It is true that I have refused to obey the orders of the Scientific Mission, in spite of the fact that my commanding officer ordered me to do so. It is true that I made a serious attempt to break the neck of the Scientific Mission's chairman, Doctor Harold Dolittle. It is also true that I sincerely regret this attempt.

"I hold nothing personal against Doctor Dolittle. Scientists have been playing at exterminating the human race for centuries and it's probably only an accident that one of them hasn't succeeded before now. And since Doctor Dolittle actually has succeeded, breaking his neck would not help the situation. It was bound to happen sooner or later, anyway.

"When I was a kid back in Minnesota, there was a boy on our street named Fitzharris Holloway. We all called him Fizz and he wasn't a bad kid except that he was just too curious to live. Let a bunch of us stand around a puddle and it would always be Fizz who would drop a big rock and splash mud all over our Sunday clothes and get the lot of us whipped. He'd drop it just to see what would happen. The average mentality could figure that out without the experiment, but Fizz's mentality wasn't average. It was scientific.

He had to see for himself. Let us find a hornets' nest and it would be Fizz who had to punch a stick into it. He'd get stung, of course, but so would the rest of us.

"You've heard that old gag about throwing an egg into an electric fan? Almost everyone has, I guess, and been satisfied just to hear it. But Fizz had to see for himself. He got egg splashed all over himself and his ma's new dress, and he wore a pillow to his meals for the next three days.

"They'll never forget Fizz at old Central High School. The scars he left in that chemistry laboratory will last as long as the building. All the teacher had to say was, 'Don't do this.' And there would be Fizz out in the lab trying it out.

"I figure now that Fizz was just a natural-born scientist. Most of us are curious about things as children—curious within limits, that is—but we outgrow it. A scientist never outgrows it, and the law of averages gives us a certain number of irresponsible scientists. Fizz met his end in a bar one night, when he dropped a lighted cigarette into the bulging front of a woman's dress. She picked up a bottle and broke it over his head, and the jury called it justifiable homicide. If all natural-born scientists had run squarely into the consequences of their curiosity at such an early age, the human race might be no further along than the Bronze Age, but at least it would have a future.

"I attempted to resign my Space Navy commission when I first learned that I was to assist Doctor Dolittle in his experiments. Contrary to normal procedure, my resignation was not accepted. I am now requesting permission to resign and join the start colonists. They have an opening for a reserve pilot and will favorably consider my application. I believe the risks of star colonization to be considerably less than those of remaining in this solar system. Doctor Dolittle has been poking at a hornets' nest, and the more light-years away I am when the hornets come out, the better I'll like it.

"Respectfully yours, Captain Paul Paulson."

* * * *

Captain Front stroked his check thoughtfully. "So they let him go. And then, two months after the colonists left, this happened. What sort of experiments was this Scientific Mission carrying on?"

"The only thing I could find was Grandfather's statement."

"I wonder if they were conducting some kind of solar experiments. I never thought of the sun as being a hornets' nest. What comes out when you poke a sun?"

"Grandfather was attached to the Jupiter Base Command, on Callisto. We might find more information there. Any chance of hitting Callisto again on the way out?'

"We'll see what we find here. If this looks like a likely clue, we'll have to follow it up. So far, there haven't been any other clues. Let's see what Walter says about this."

* * * *

Vainly they searched such mute records as Earth had to offer. They sifted the bones of the Venus colonists and looked in at Mercury Base, where death had interrupted the lonely vigil of a small group of scientists and soldiers. Then they turned back. Mars again, then an asteroid base, and then Callisto.

And the complete file on Captain Paul Paulson.

Paulson searched further and found the records of the Scientific Mission. He carried an armload of document to Captain Front.

"Found any answers?" the captain asked.

"Not all of them," Paulson said, "but enough."

"Solar research?"

"No. Jupiter research."

"Odd," the captain mused. "Whatever happened hit everything from the Jupiter moons through the system clear to Mercury."

"This Doctor Dolittle," Paulson said, "was doing some intensified research that concerned Jupiter. First, he used a series of atomic warheads to test the depth of the atmosphere. Then he wanted someone to pilot a ship on a tight parabolic orbit that would take him closer to Jupiter than any human had ever been before. As an added twist, the ship was to be paralleled closer in by a guided missile that could broadcast instrument readings. Grandfather Paulson was ordered to pilot the ship. He refused. He was tried for insubordination, convicted and sentenced to a prison term."

"But he left with the star colonists."

"Yes, by escaping from confinement. He got out to Pluto Base and stowed away on the starship. Jupiter Command was furious when it found out what had happened. The commandant ordered the starship to turn around and bring him back. The starship was out of the system then and it refused."

"Well, that's an interesting bit of family history, but it doesn't explain what wiped out humanity."

Paulson said grimy, "Doesn't it?"

"Does it?"

"Grandfather Paulson said Doctor Dolittle had been poking at a hornets' nest. He was poking at Jupiter, and it was vigorous poking—he used atomic warheads. Then, when Grandfather refused to pilot Dolittle's ship, Dolittle found another pilot who would. They went into their orbit and made the trip successfully, but they lost their guided missile. Then, a few weeks later, they found it again."

* * * *

Captain Front said blankly, "They lost it on Jupiter—and then they found it?"

"The missile came shooting back at them," said Paulson. "I gather that it was only a piece of luck that let them capture it, because the mechanism had been altered in a way they called 'astonishing,' and it used an unknown fuel. Its speed was something they couldn't believe. It represented several hundred years' progress for them at one crack, and it gave them the secret of star travel. They went to work on it, and they were too enthused to give much thought to what else might come up from Jupiter."

The captain walked over to a port and looked out at the sky. "*Jupiter?*"

"It must have been hell for something native to Jupiter to take to space travel, but someone—or something—was as mad as a hornet. Atomic warheads wouldn't soothe anyone's feelings."

"So it—or they—headed toward the sun."

"At unbelievable speeds," Paulson said. "Those on the outer planets either had time to try to escape, or maybe to come to help."

"And all the humanity they could find—how did they do it?"

"I hope we never know. How did they ever get off Jupiter? Not even our starship could manage that. What's the escape velocity?"

"Too much."

"Well, I found the study they made of the missile. It's an advance in mankind's knowledge—at the price of mankind."

"I'll have Walter go over it."

"Where is he?" Paulson asked. "I haven't seen him for days."

The captain stiffened. "My God! He's down on Amalthea, conducting some Jupiter experiments!"

* * * *

The desolate rock-strewn surface of Amalthea curved sharply away from them to its shallow horizon and the light in the sky was Jupiter. The huge disc of the planet hovered menacingly above them

The churning bands of clouds writhed and struggled like live beings in the throes of mortal agony. Even as they watched, the colors deepened and faded, yellow clouds boiled into the brown of the North Equatorial Belt, and the enigmatic, so-called *red* spot shimmered with a repulsive, grayish pinkness.

"Grandfather must have had come kind of apprehension about it," Paulson said. "Just the sight of it is enough to scare a man to death. I feel as if it were going to gobble me up."

He turned expectantly to Doctor Walter, and the scientist said nothing. Behind the tinted thickness of his face-plate, his eyes bulged and sparkled.

"I feel," Paulson said, "as if I were on a disabled ship that is likely to crash at any second."

The scientist took a step forward—toward Jupiter. "Out, damned spot!" he muttered. "Out, I say!"

Paulson jumped, and came down slowly. "How was that again?"

"Shakespeare," the scientist said.

"I said I feel as if I were on a disabled ship—"

"I heard you. Nonsense. It's true that this little moon is falling toward Jupiter, but it's only an inch and a fraction a year. Fifty million years from now, it'll be a few miles closer. Eventually it'll go all the way but *you* won't be around to worry about it."

"No one will be around to worry about it," Paulson said. "Do you think someone down there will think it's another bombardment when the moon falls, and come up to see who did it?"

Walter said shortly, "I wouldn't know."

"You have to admit that was a stupid way to experiment on an unknown planet. Atomic warheads!"

"Who would have imagined anything could be living down there?" Walter said.

"But what could they learn?"

"I'm sure they had some definite objective. You don't think they did it just for the fun of it, do you?"

Paulson turned, "Your hour's up. Let's get going."

They made long, slow-motion bounds across the crumbling surface. Suddenly Paulson missed Walter, and turned to find him motionless, staring at Jupiter.

"You said an hour was all you wanted," Paulson said sharply. "We're jumping off at midnight, you know, and I only have half the computations made."

"All right," Walter said. "I was just looking."

* * * *

When they reached the tiny lifeship. Walter turned again, before he entered the airlock. "I'd give a lot to know what's down there. With all the study that Scientific Mission put in, they really found out nothing about the planet."

"I can tell you how to manage it," said Paulson.

"How?"

"Give us about a six-month start. Then fly down and see for yourself. We'll leave you the lifeship."

Walter turned abruptly and entered the airlock.

Paulson followed him. "Sure, it's a fascinating thing," he said. "And I'm glad the planets in our own solar systems run Earth-normal and smaller. Otherwise, some scientist might decide to conduct some experiments. I'm glad Jupiter is light-years away from my home town, but after this I'll never feel easy about it. Who can say that they won't come out again someday, and take to star traveling?"

They took off, and Paulson set course for Callisto Base. A moment later Walter got up and left the control section. When Paulson got curious and went back to look for him, he found the scientist pressing his face against a porthole, staring at Jupiter.

MATING INSTINCT

First published in *Super-Science Fiction*, June 1959

Mazie Perkins ate her lunch stoically and kept her nose in her plate. The tittering voices from the next booth were burning lashes that ripped at her bent shoulders.

"I'm worried about Mazie."

"What's she done now?"

"It's about Charlie Rawson. He threw her over, you know."

"She said she threw him over."

"What would you expect her to say? She isn't getting any younger, but she still has some pride left."

"That was a couple of weeks ago, wasn't it? Don't tell me she's still moping. She's been thrown over before. She ought to be used to it."

"She was pretty far gone on Charlie."

"Say—you don't suppose she's…"

The titters erupted wildly.

"Time will tell. But now she's really gone off the deep end. Know what she told me this morning? She's found her ideal man. It's the purest of pure love. They communicate mentally, and she's never seen him."

"Honestly! Just who is this ideal lover-boy?"

"She didn't mention his name. All she said was that he's out of this world."

Mazie picked up her check, and adroitly slipped away unseen. Outside, the wind was cold and cutting, and there was a trace of snow in the air. Another nine inches by tomorrow morning, the weather forecast said. Mazie buried her face in the narrow fur of her collar, and smiled happily to herself. She'd show them, she would—the cackling hens! Just wait until He came. He'd promised

He would come, and she believed Him. Who wouldn't believe a promise like that?

Her wind-reddened cheeks blushed a deeper red as she thought of some of the details of last night's conversation. She was certain of one thing. When her dream-man finally arrived, He would really be a lover-boy.

Superior-General Pbelaz hunched himself fore-ward on his cushion, and idly coiled lower left around upper right. "It looks promising," he admitted. "Just now it's the most promising thing we have. But it's too far—much too far. Keep a file on it, and perhaps after the next jump it will be within range.

Inferior-General Pnarar gestured appealingly with middle left and right. "It would be a shame to waste it. Pkalir seems to have an excellent connection, and he's making good progress. Why not let him follow it up?"

"Too far," Superior-General Pbelaz said. "Too risky. I hope you haven't forgotten the Plaoz disaster. We only exceeded the safe range by seventeen percent that time. This one would be at least thirty per cent. It isn't worth the risk, no matter how promising the world might be."

"But—hoping you will excuse the foolish obstinacy—this case has some unusual aspects. Would you consent to discuss it with Pkalir?"

Superior-General Pbelaz uncoiled and coiled again. "If it is a truly unusual case, there could be no harm in discussing it. Certainly there is little we can do but talk, until our next objective is defined. You may send for Pkalir."

Inferior-General Pnarar bowed deeply, and fluttered upper left and right. "I have Pkalir waiting outside."

Communications Technician Pkalir, elite grade, entered the room confidently. Generals did not awe him. He rubbed uppers with the generals every day, and he'd never met one who could channel a thought beam with his dexterity. The Superior-General was hardly in the same class with lesser officers, but even so…

Pkalir bowed, and snappily saluted with upper and middle left. Inferior-General Pnarar made the presentation. Superior-General Pbelaz relaxed on his cushion, and ordered Pkalir to tell him just what it was about this distant planet that was different.

"The name of the planet," Pkalir said, "is Earth. Using the native terminology, of course."

"Awkward," Superior-General Pbelaz mused. "We must change it. Supposing we shortened it to Pbert?"

"As you wish, sir," Pkalir said. "I am accumulating data upon this planet Pbert as rapidly as possible. It seems to be a most desirable planet, thought of course my data is by no means complete. The unusual feature is the nature of the contact. It seems the dominant species of the planet possesses two sexes."

Superior-General Pbelaz intertwined upper, middle and lower left and right, and shuddered, "Utterly disgusting!"

"It does seem a bit incredible," Inferior-General Pnarar said. "Are you certain that your contact is reliable? We have had instances, you know, when a contact deliberately misled."

Pkalir favored the generals with a smile, which he managed to keep humble. "My contact is absolutely reliable. May I proceed?"

"Please do," the Superior-General said.

"The two sexes are labeled, and evidently for purposes of identification, man and woman, boy and girl, male and female. The terms are used interchangeably. My contact is of the female class. Now I hardly need to remind your Excellencies of the motivation which we invariably develop in our contacts."

"Greed," Superior-General Pbelaz said.

"Wealth, power—anything else we must promise to insure their cooperation in betraying their fellow creatures. Greed, of course. But this contact is different. As a motivating factor, greed would be worthless. The world is incredibly rich, and the contact seems to have all desires fulfilled except one."

Pkalir paused, and the Superior-General waved lower left impatiently: "Go on."

"The contact desires a mate."

"Mate? Surely you don't mean to say…"

"Pardon, your Excellency, but it is a fact. There are two sexes, and the compulsion to reproduction is an exceedingly powerful one, as any of us can testify. With two sexes, reproduction cannot be achieved without a mate. I believe that this contact is more forcefully motivated that any contact I can remember. It balances off the distance factor, you see."

"Interesting. But I assure you, it will require a monumental amount of proof to convince me that I should disregard the distance factor."

Pkalir extended middle right, and placed a file before Superior-General. "I have asked Exotic Research for information on duo-sexuality. There is a surprising amount of it—even on this world. It doesn't occur among dominant species, of course, or even intelligent species, but it's all around us if we care to observe it."

The superior-General opened the file. "Interesting. Let's see. Where there are two sexes, the desire to mate with a creature of the opposite sex is one of the basic instincts. Logical, and therefore probably true. Exotic Research wouldn't dare send a mistake in here. What you mean, Pkalir, is that you are appealing to this contact's mating instinct. The contact believes that you—insufferable pzarlassis!"

Pkalir purpled gently. "True. The contact considers me a potential mate. I have sorted out the thought-images and projected back to the contact a composite of the most ideal of all ideal mates—from the contact's point-of-view, of course. The situation seems most advantageous."

"It does, indeed." The Superior-General conceded. "You have my permission to explore the possibilities of the planet Pbert. Naturally I do not commit myself to any course of action at this time, but I shall study your future reports with interest."

"Until our next conference…" Inferior-General Pnarar suggested.

"Certainly. Until our next conference…" He dismissed them with a double-snap of lower right.

Mazie felt the same churning uncertainty which she always felt when she was about to commune with Him. She knew that the first time had been an accident, and unworthy as she was, that the accident had made her the most fortunate of all women. She had been bitter and lonely, and as she stood in her window looking sadly out at the clear night sky, a certain star caught her attention. She had willed all of her loneliness and longing directly at that star.

And He had answered. It had been a miracle out of nothing, out of emptiness.

He had made her understand that the star was her guide. She had to will her thoughts directly at it, and even on a clear night she might come distressingly near to failure. It was the smokestack that saved her. It pointed its looming black finger directly at the star. She had but to look at the smoke stack, raise her eyes slightly, and there it was, waiting for her.

She did not often succeed the first time. She was coming to understand that space was vast, and that a pin point of error might make worlds of difference out by her favorite star.

The night was overcast. Even the smoke stack was nearly obscured by the driving snow. Wind rattled the window and sent cold eddies swirling about her. She raised her eyes, just…about…there. "Hello, up there. Hello. Are you there?"

There was no response. Bravely she shifted her position a little, only a very little, and tried again. "Hello, up there. Hello. Are you there?"

The booming thought seemed to fill the room. "Hello. Hello, dream-girl. Are you there?"

"I'm here," she thought back at Him. She relaxed, and waited.

They had their usual preliminary love talk, when the thoughts she received seemed to mirror her own deepest desires. And then, as usual, he began to question her. What sort of a world did she live on? He'd have to know, if he were to join her. Was it hot there? No, she told him. It wasn't hot. Was it cold? She shivered as the snow pelted her window. No, it wasn't cold. It was just right. Perfect. It would be even more perfect when He came.

Was it dangerous there? Did people have weapons? Was there plenty of food? What kind of dwellings did the people use? How did the people travel? Was there plenty of—water, that was the word—was there enough of it?

She clutched her dressing gown tightly about her, and lied cheerfully. She described a paradise, a utopia—Mazie Perkin's utopia—where the climate was always balmy, where people dwelt in harmonious luxury, where the only unfulfilled desire was the desire for a mate, because men were fickle and chose to wander.

"Are you coming?" she asked. "When are you coming?"

"Soon. I'm coming soon. But first I must test you."

"Test? What sort of test?"

"I'll tell you next time. It isn't difficult. Next time…"

Mazie went off to bed, and dreamed of the blond, handsome male, of tender, affectionate disposition and sturdy physique, whose mental image reached out to her from the stars.

"There is more water than land on Pbert," Pkalir said. "Since the temperature seems to be uniform everywhere, my conclusion is that the landmass lies mainly in the same thermal zone."

"You say the contact calls the temperature ideal," Superior-General Pbelaz said. "Ideal from the contact's point-of-view may not be ideal from our point-of-view."

"True. The contact says it is always about eighty degrees, which means nothing. However, I found that the temperature scale is based upon properties of water and ranges from thirty-two degrees for freezing to two hundred twelve for boiling. That still doesn't tell us much. I've made an allowance for pressure, and it comes out…"

The Superior-General winced. "A little on the cold side."

"Not seriously so."

"No, if it doesn't vary too much from this eighty-degree norm, we could manage. You're still certain contact is reliable?"

"Absolutely."

"Well then—what about defenses?"

"They seem to have none. Evidently all the enemies of the dominant species were destroyed long ago, and the society is uniquely peaceful. I believe we can count upon no opposition."

"That makes for a cursedly uninteresting invasion," the Superior-General growled, waving middle and lower left disgustedly. "Still—it makes a good jump for us. The Boya Majesty will be pleased. Now if we can be certain the contact can be relied upon, we can proceed with our planning."

"The mating instinct can be relied upon," Pkalir said. "I shall conduct the usual tests, of course. But I am confident. Has your Excellency studied the material provided by Exotic Research?"

"I have," the Superior-General said. "I am ready to concede that the mating instinct is an uncommonly powerful thing. Even so, I shall insist upon the most rigid tests and an adequate safety factor."

"I don't think there will be any difficulty," Pkalir said. "The contact wants a mate rather badly."

Mazie was tense with excitement. She was also worried. She had never been very good at tests, and now she had to take a test with her entire future happiness depending upon the outcome. So certain she was of failure that her sense of direction became confused. It took her nearly an hour to make contact, and she was sobbing with desperation when the answering thought enveloped and comforted her.

She was quickly reassured. The test was simply an endurance test.

"I shall have to come a long way to find you," the thought told her. "You must send your thoughts to me so I can follow them back to you. If you stop even for an instant I shall be lost. We will never see each other, and I will not be able…"

The details were embarrassingly explicit. Mazie blushed furiously in the darkness of her room, and swore she would not under any circumstances cut off her thoughts.

* * * *

"How long will it take?" she asked.

"I cannot tell you. I know approximately how far I must come, but I do not measure time as you do. You must take the test, and continue until I tell you to stop. Then you will know."

"When should I start?"

"Whenever you are ready."

"I think—maybe I should find a chair."

She placed the chair carefully, and seated herself, and regained contact. This night the sky was clear, and the multitude of stars hung low over her window. Her particular star—His star—winked at her familiarly. Were there any special thoughts he wanted her to think? It did not matter, He said. The important thing was that she continue to think.

With the glow of inner satisfaction she sat erect in her chair. Mazie Perkins, heroine, braving the storm-swept beach to swing her lantern and guide the ship to safety. Mazie Perkins, modern heroine, sending out a radio beacon to a far-off, unseen, unheard plane in distress.

She recited poetry and nursery rhymes and taught herself the alphabet backwards. She practiced the multiplication tables and wearily droned all the endearments she would say to Him when he arrived. It was only six o'clock when she started, and the evening crept interminably into night, and the night dragged mockingly. She did not dare break her flow of thought to steal glances at the clock. From far away the sound of church bells marked off the hours, and she could not even disturb her concentration to count them.

Vaguely she realized that it was getting very late. Traffic noises died down. Lights flicked off in nearby houses. She began to feel terribly sleepy.

She started as his thoughts broke in upon hers. She was doing marvelous, He told her. He thought that she had reached the halfway mark. She brightened, and kept going with a new determination.

She was half-dead with weariness when He finally told her she could stop. She had done nobly, He said. There would have to be another test, and maybe two more, but now there was no longer any doubt. He would be joining her—soon.

Her happiness was lyrical as she tumbled into bed. It was three A. M.

With a nonchalance which he did not feel, Pkalir took his position in the control center of the Command Ship. It was not the first time he had occupied the lofty post of Thought Leader, but it was by far the most important time. The Superior-General was present, along with a vast multitude of lesser officers, but Pkalir was the real commander. Until they broke atmosphere at their destination planet, at Pbert, he controlled the Command ship, and through it, the fleet.

It was the longest jump the Imperial Forces had attempted in long ages of interplanetary conquest. If it succeeded, Pkalir would be a general himself—perhaps as soon as the new conquest was made secure. If it failed…

One did not think about failure on a mission such as this. One made certain beforehand that there could be no failure. He was certain of his contact, and once they broke atmosphere the powerful fleet and the armed forces could handle any emergency.

Staff-General Pcodaz watched alertly as Pkalir checked his instruments. He was commanding officer of the Communications Technicians, and he was, Pkalir thought, more than a little jealous over Pkalir's position on this jump. He had opposed the project from the start, and even ordered Pkalir to abandon his contact. Fortunately Pkalir had been able to interest Inferior-General Pnarar.

But the Staff-General remained unconvinced. "You're certain of this contact of yours?" Pkalir carefully corrected an instrument setting with middle left. "Certain."

"It could be a trap, you know."

'Impossible. The contact believes there will be one more test. Even if it were a trap, the contact would not attempt it on a test. The trap would come on the next thought-run, and of course there will not be any. We will be there."

"I wasn't referring to the thought-run. I was referring to the military operation. I can't imagine an intelligent species with two sexes, either."

"I think the Superior-General is uneasy about it. I have never seen him make such detailed preparations."

"So much the better," Pkalir said. "If there is a trap, we'll spring it. That's for the military to worry about. All I'm going to concentrate on is the thought-run."

Though he did not dare admit it, he was becoming uneasy about the same question. Was it possible that a planet could be completely defenseless? They had encountered fantastic weapons in the worlds they conquered but always before the contact had supplied detailed descriptions of all weapons, and his contact did not know about them.

The Staff-General said, with a vaguely insulting smile, "What will your contact say when you arrive? Will it still be interested in mating after it sees you?"

"I know what *it* looks like," Pkalir said, "and I'm surprised that the species has any offspring at all."

The Superior-General vaulted in, and checked the control lights. "Everything ready?"

"Everything ready," Pkalir said.

The Superior-General brought out a flask and wound it with upper right. "To our new planet." "To our new planet," they repeated, and the Superior-General drank.

A light flashed, and Pkalir was instantly alert. He flashed back a thought. "Hello, dream-girl. A little early, aren't you?"

"I got home early tonight. I'm glad you didn't try it again last night. I was awfully tired."

"Are you feeling up to it tonight?"

"I feel fine tonight."

"Wonderful. Just this one last test, dear-one, and the next time I'll be on my way to you. You won't let me down, will you?"

"Of course not. I did all right before, didn't I?"

"You were perfect. But this is the last test, and it's a very important one."

"Should I start now?"

The Superior-General had taken his position. Behind him, Pkalir could see the officers and technicians making ready. "Not yet. Let's talk for a little while. I have things to say to you."

The Superior-General was rechecking his battle plans. Pkalir could see that he was suspicious of the idea of a defenseless planet. He was certain that the creatures would have some kind of weapon. Pkalir flapped upper left and right idly. Let the Superior-General worry about that. That was his job—to worry. He did precious little else.

He concentrated on his contact, projecting back at it all of the disgusting ideas which he had filtered out of its thoughts. At first the procedure had sickened him. Now he could go through the motions without entangling lower left and right, but it still left him feeling uncomfortable.

Ready lights flashed around him. At his left, his assistant was working the large control panel that cleared the other ships. The lights were coming on one by one. The Superior-General went over to check. When the last lights flashed, he waved upper right at Pkalir and vaulted back to his position.

"All ready," he said slyly. "Is your contact ready to mate?"

"Ready, dear-one?" Pkalir flashed.

"Just a minute—I'll get the chair. There. Now I'm ready."

"We'll start the test now. Remember that I'm counting on you. Don't let me down. And I promise—this is the last test."

"I hope so! But you can depend on me. You know that."

The thought-reading was firm and clear. Pkalir made a few final adjustments, glanced at the Staff-General, and tremulously extended upper left for the launching lever. He pulled it, and was jerked into blackness.

It was the way it always had been and the way it had to be. A complex living organism could not function at the tremendous acceleration essential to stellar travel. At slower speeds there could be no stellar travel.

Solution: send mental fingers probing across the depths of space. Locate an intelligent creature on another world. Bribe that creature to continuously maintain-thought contact. Lock the stellar ships on that thought-beacon. Let the entire fleet travel the thought-run with all personnel in a state of physical and mental inertness. The tremendous acceleration no longer mattered. There were no navigation problems. The automatic deceleration devices cut in as the run neared its end. If it were an invasion fleet, another world was ready for conquest—a surprise conquest.

It was a superb plan. It was perfect. It worked. It had conquered worlds without number. After victory it was not even necessary to pay the bribe, unless the commanding general felt inclined to generosity.

Of all the thousands that made up the personnel of the invading force, only the Thought-Leader had to be active during the run. Pkalir lay supine on his cushion, upper, middle and lower left and right frozen in contact with his instruments, his body a shimmering, jellified mass under the tortuous strain. He strove for a hazy form of mental alertness. He could rely upon the instruments—nothing could go wrong there. But it was considered wise, if not necessary, to occasionally reassure the contact.

"You're doing fine, dear-one. You're marvelous. You're the most."

"I wondered if you were still there. Mary had a little lamb, its fleece was white and green and purple and orange…

The thought droned on and on. The contact really was doing an excellent job. Pkalir relaxed and listened, and then reluctantly stirred himself again. Already they had come a quarter of the distance, he estimated.

He squirmed into such a position of comfort as he could manage, and congratulated himself. This would be a history-making expedition. It developed an entirely new principle of conquest. Soon communications technicians all through the far-flung empire would be searching for planets where the mating instinct could be exploited. Perhaps it would be called the Pkalir Technique. He would be asked to prepare a manual, to explain its use.

Suddenly his instruments went dead. A bell sounded. Lights flashed. Pkalir waited patiently. Even the best contact suffered moments of mental blankness.

He sent out a reassuring thought. "Still here, dear-one. You're doing fine."

There was no response.

Pkalir's thoughts assumed a note of urgency. "Don't let me down, dear-one. Are you there? Try a little harder. You're not coming through."

Still there was no response.

Pkalir's middle right tightened on the emergency alert. The Superior-General gave him a look of tortured alarm. By his side, the Staff-General twisted in panic.

"I'm—swinging three left," Pkalir announced . "Then I'll swing six right. Perhaps I can pick it up."

"Concur," the Superior-General said.

The Staff-General whined his approval. Pkalir completed the maneuver. His instruments remained dead.

The Superior-General activated his own controls. "Is it completely lost?" He asked.

"It's—gone," Pkalir admitted. He shuddered, seeing his entire career crashing in ruins about him.

"We'll circle." The Superior-General said, "Until we pick up the emergency thought-beacon from base. We're fortunate this happened this soon, of it had to happen."

The strain rippled in his face as he made the adjustment. Maneuvering at top acceleration was no simple matter, especially since it had to be done do rarely. Pkalir watched him uneasily. He could not remember ever having been caught in space without thought-contact.

They were well into the maneuver when the general alarm clattered urgently. With a hideous scream the Superior-General slammed at the emergency deceleration control.

Pkalir had a glimpse at the screen before the sudden shock slammed him into unconsciousness, and that glimpse was enough to tell him they were lost. The Command Ship, and the fleet it led were streaking at top acceleration directly into a sun.

"Here's Mazie," one of the girls said. "Hey, Mazie—how are you making out with your dream man?"

Mazie sniffed. "Oh, him. I cut him out."

"I thought you were pretty well gone on him. Just yesterday you were telling me what hot stuff he is."

"Hot stuff—phooey," Mazie said. "All he wanted me to do was sit in front of a cold window and think. For hours, he wanted me to do that. I got fed up with it. Anyway, Charlie Rawson came around last night. He had a couple of tickets, so I let the dream man go, and went to the fights."

THE MADDER THEY COME

First published in *Fantastic*, June 1958

Doctor Stanley Hollinger was in a mild hurry, that Monday afternoon. It was a fine September day, and there was a new nurse over in the Out-Patient Division. He had not met her, but he'd glimpsed her that morning, from a distance. She was shapely, she had flaming red hair, and she flashed the kind of mocking little smile that affects men in odd ways. It affected Stanley Hollinger in just the right way, and he had no intention of letting the sun go down without getting to know her better.

He went down the hallway at a brisk trot, unlocked a door, and stepped through. A heinous bedlam smote him in the face, and he carefully closed the door behind him, and locked it. "Three wards to go," he told himself. And then the redhead. He wondered if she would be busy that night. He restrained his urge to concentrate on the patients. It took some effort.

Most of the staff doctors rarely bothered with ward visits, but Hollinger felt differently about it. A patient's behavior out in a ward often gave him some insight he never could have gleaned in his office. He brushed aside the memory of the redhead's smile, and stood looking about him with detached professional interest.

His first impression was that Ward Fifteen was quieter than usual, and that vaguely disturbed him. Not that there was any lack of noise about him. Screams, shouts and verbal explosions cut the air above the general hubbub. In the far corner, a swarthy little fellow had bribed or coerced three fellow patients into forming an audience, and they squatted on the floor in front of him while he howled at them hysterically. There was a singer in the center of the room who stopped every few notes and bowed almost correctly. A frail, middle-aged man was straining heroically to get a polisher started. He perspired, he moaned and grunted, and his face had a feverish flush. In front of him, a giant of a man was helping him out by bellowing encouragement while he hauled laboriously on an invisible rope. The polisher remained motionless.

Charlie Andrews, the robust, good-natured attendant, walked over to Hollinger and nodded politely. "Afternoon, Doctor Hollinger."

"Good afternoon, Charlie," Hollinger said.

He glanced about the room again—at the card game, where one player had most of the deck fanned out in his hand and two players concentrated intently upon no cards at all, at the sleeping forms scattered about haphazardly on the floor, at the morose patients who huddled on the wooden benches and stared vacantly into some remote dimension. One patient had managed to stretch out on a bench and two patients were sitting on top of him, and none of the three seemed to mind.

Suddenly Hollinger understood the apparent quietness. The piano was silent.

"Where's the musician?" he said.

"He can't play today. He has a broken finger—he says."

Hollinger nodded, and picked out the musician—ex-musician—among the bench sitters. He was a young man who had been a promising pianist, and he'd worked out a brilliant harmonization of *America* which seemed to be mainly atonal. At least, it sounded atonal after an hour or two of uninterrupted repetitions.

"Same old thing, eh, Charlie?" Hollinger said.

"It sure is," Charlie said.

Hollinger shrugged. He'd only been at the Cardale State Hospital for six months, but a staff member became quickly inured to the extraordinary. If he did not, the chances were excellent that he would stop being a staff member, and better than average that he would find himself well on the way to meeting the rather stiff entrance qualifications imposed upon the patients.

"Well . . ." Hollinger said, turning to leave. He stopped. "Where'd they get the broom?"

Charlie whirled, and swore savagely. "Now who smuggled that in here?"

He bounded forward, and Hollinger called sharply to him. "Wait!"

A chubby, white-haired man had the broom up in the air, trying to balance it on his nose. He steadied it, took away his hands, and ducked awkwardly as it crashed to the floor. Undaunted, he raised it again. The other patients ignored him.

"Sidney Carter, isn't it?" Hollinger said.

"Yeah," Charlie said. "That is Sid, all right."

The broom crashed down a second time, and a third. Hollinger kept count, his clinical curiosity aroused. How many failures would Sidney Carter tolerate before he lost interest?

The broom came down a fourth time, and whacked Carter soundly on the head as it fell. He picked it up, and studied it with an air of mystification.

"Shall I take it away from him?" Charlie asked.

"Wait," Hollinger said.

The broom went up again, was steadied, released, and—stayed. Carter staggered about wildly, body arched back, nose erect, and somehow kept the broom in the air. He regained his equilibrium, and boldly started a triumphant circuit of the room. Another patient followed along behind, mimicking his contorted posture and jerky movements.

The procession had gone twenty feet, and was picking up speed, when Carter walked out from under the broom. He did not immediately notice this oversight. He kept moving forward, back arched, nose erect. Hollinger forgot Carter, and concentrated on the broom—because the broom did not seem to notice the oversight, either. It hung in mid-air, motionlessly perpendicular, and Carter's mimic strutted under it, grinned at the sight of it hovering over him, and moved on.

Ten feet away, Carter suddenly missed the broom. He straightened up with a look of profound surprise on his round face, and turned just in time to see the broom plummet downwards.

"Did you see that?" Hollinger muttered.

"No," Charlie said. "No—I don't think that I did."

On his way back to his office, Hollinger encountered the red-headed nurse in the hallway. He passed her without so much as a nod.

That evening Hollinger and Charlie Andrews sat in the comfortable quarters of Doctor Willard Manley, the hospital's Associate Director. Hollinger told the story, and Doctor Manley listened, and gazed peacefully at the fire that crackled in the fireplace, and stirred himself only to refill their glasses. His twitching eyebrows registered just the proper amount of incredulity, and he said nothing.

"You act," Hollinger said, "as if you don't believe us."

"I don't."

"Why not? We were both there. We both saw it."

"I'm glad the Doc was there," Charlie broke in. "If it was just me that saw it, I'd of never mentioned it."

"Exactly," Doctor Manley said. "One hears about so many queer things around a place like this."

Hollinger exploded. "We're not patients, damn it!"

"No!" Manley admitted, cocking his bald head as if he thought that condition could be corrected easily enough. "You say you saw it. Now what do you want to do about it?"

"I was going to suggest that we give Carter a broom tomorrow, and you watch yourself and see what happens."

"All right," Doctor Manley said. "I will. Ordinarily I refuse to dignify an irrational experiment by my presence; but it's obvious that I'll have to get to the bottom of this thing, Hollinger, if there's going to be any work done in your section this week."

Hollinger winced, and afterwards he was rather glad that his response had been inaudible.

The following morning Doctors Manley and Hollinger waited unobtrusively in one corner of the room, while Charlie Andrews handed a broom to Sidney Carter. They watched as Carter solemnly swept his way around the room twice, energetically sending up clouds of imaginary dust. Eventually Carter dropped the broom and wandered away. Another patient picked it up, straddled it, and galloped about uttering piercing whoops. When he discarded it and slumped panting to the floor, a third patient seized it, raised it to his shoulder, and carefully shot the musician, who was beginning his hundred and tenth rendition of *America*. The musician whirled when his fellow patient shouted, "Bang!" He walked over and jerked the broom out of his hands, laid it down on the floor, and returned to the piano.

"At least the fellow still has some critical faculty," Doctor Manley murmured.

A patient left the card table, grabbed the broom, and made like a baton twirler. The broom handle struck the floor its first time around, and the broom fluttered away. Sidney Carter picked it up, and resumed his sweeping.

Doctor Manley grunted disgustedly. "This is where I came in."

"Give him a chance," Hollinger said.

Carter slid the broom across the floor, and joined the kibitzers around the card game. He leaned over and coyly studied the hand of a player who held no cards.

"Let me try something," Charlie said. He picked up the broom and held it in the air, over his head. Carter saw him and hurried back, babbling excitedly. Charlie handed him the broom, and slowly edged away from him. Hollinger took out a stop watch, and waited.

On Carter's third try the broom stayed up. He gave a nasal shout of triumph, and staggered away. He negotiated half-a-dozen steps safely, stumbled over a sleeping patient, and lost his balance. Hollinger clicked his stop watch, and waited breathlessly. The broom remained in the air, swinging slowly, like a pendulum.

Carter landed heavily on his rear. For a few seconds he sat looking about foolishly. Then he remembered his broom. He finally located it, and scrambled to his feet just as it slid slowly floorward.

Hollinger clicked his stop watch again.

"How long?" Doctor Manley asked.

"Eighteen seconds."

"It seemed like a week. Let's get out of here."

Charlie let them out, and locked the door after them. They strolled down the dingy hallway, unlocked another door, and stepped out into the bright fall sunshine. Doctor Manley led the way across the hospital grounds to a bench. They sat down, lit cigarettes, and looked out on a quiet residential street.

"Telekinesis," Doctor Manley said.

"It has to be," Hollinger admitted.

"So much has been written about the so-called *psi* powers, both fact and fiction. At one time in the past the subject—ah—interested me. I remember tales of good people using *psi* powers benevolently, and bad people using *psi* powers fiendishly. But I don't recall anything about an insane person having them. What does he use them for? What possible benefit could such powers be to him, or to anyone else? Good and bad are only relative terms, you know, but this person could be dangerous. So what do we do about it? Nail everything down, and forget it?"

"I honestly don't know," Hollinger said.

"I think we have an obligation," Manley said thoughtfully. "An obligation to study and experiment. If we can find out who it is, of course."

Hollinger turned quickly. "Who it is? But Carter . . ."

"Not Carter. Think back on the way he reacted. Someone helped him balance the broom, and held it up when he fell. How many men do you have in that ward?"

"Thirty-four."

"Thirty-three, then, not counting Carter. And not one of them is rational enough to cooperate. Now how do we find out who it is?"

"I still think it's Carter. He was concentrating mentally on keeping the broom up, and that kind of mental effort must be the basis for telekinesis. Of course, he wouldn't know that his mental effort was responsible. But I'll give you odds he was the only one concentrating on it. No one else paid any attention to him."

"It's impossible to say just where a patient's attention might be," Doctor Manley said testily. "Anyway, we can't settle the problem by arguing about it. Now let's think of some tests, and get back in there and apply them."

They isolated Sidney Carter and his broom, and Carter refused to perform. He sat sullenly on the floor, his round face drooping mournfully, and muttered unintelligibilities to himself. He brightened when half a dozen of his fellow patients were placed with him. A short time later he was balancing the broom, and Hollinger clocked it suspended in mid-air for fourteen seconds.

"That's a piece of luck," Doctor Manley said. "Got him the first try. Now we'll remove one patient at a time, until the broom stops balancing."

"Wait a minute," Hollinger objected. "This doesn't prove it isn't Carter. It may just prove that Carter won't perform without company."

"I still think—but then, you may be right."

"We need a control. Another group of six or seven."

"I suppose it wouldn't do any harm," Doctor Manley admitted.

They brought in a second group, and a third, and a fourth and fifth. And Sidney Carter continued his balancing act, and at some point in each performance the broom defied gravity. Hollinger clock a record thirty-two-second suspension.

Manley and Hollinger returned the patients to Ward Fifteen, and walked back across the hospital grounds to their bench.

"Don't look so damned smug," Manley snapped.

"Sir?" Hollinger said innocently.

"All right. So it *has* to be Carter. Either that, or there's at least five of them. And that is impossible. If one human being out of a million has telekinetic ability—and I doubt that—we would hardly find five in one ward of a mental hospital."

"I was considering it from another angle," Hollinger said. "Why should we find even one in a mental hospital?"

Manley looked at him sharply. "Are you hinting at a theory? Mental unbalance a necessary prerequisite for *psi* powers?"

"Not a necessary prerequisite. A probable resultant. Look at it this way. A person who is a sensitive telepath from birth would hardly have a thought to call his own. He'd be bombarded continuously by other mentalities, and it would be impossible for him to develop normally. Even if he did maintain a slight edge of mental balance, one afternoon in Yankee Stadium would drive him violently insane."

"Your conclusion?"

"If you want to find a first rate telepath, look in a mental hospital. Of course, you'll have a hell of a time differentiating between him and the other patients."

"Telepaths are supposed to be able to shield themselves from other minds."

"That's the theory, too. Besides—would a baby be able to shield itself? Even if it had ability to shield itself, it would be a mental case before it ever learned how to use that ability."

"None of which helps us with our telekinetic patient."

"Perhaps not," Hollinger admitted. "But then—he may be a telepath too. We haven't any idea what other power he may have. And even if he isn't, unexpressed telekinetic powers could result in insanity. A person with great musical talent might become a mental case digging ditches. A person with great telekinetic talent might become a mental case if he didn't understand his telekinetic urges and didn't know what to do about them."

"Let's not lose our perspective on this," Manley said, dryly. "We have one mental patient, and we are only positive about one *psi* power. Let's check on Sidney Carter's background, and decide what to do with him."

They hurried off to the Records Section, and checked. Prior to his mental break-down, Sidney Carter had led a normal, humdrum existence. There had been no apparent foreshadowing of his mental illness. He'd been a grocery store clerk, a factory worker, and a bus driver. He'd had an apparently happy marriage, and raised three children. He'd been committed at the age of fifty-one, and he'd been a patient for twelve years, with no apparent improvement.

"If your theory's correct," Manley said, "he contained those urges pretty well for fifty-one years."

"What do we do now?"

"Supposing we were able to effect a cure by encouraging him to use his telekinetic ability? That would make medical history. This case will make medical history no matter what happens. Our next step is to teach the patients of Ward Fifteen a new game."

It took all of half an hour but Manley succeeded in getting the thirty-four patients seated on the floor in a large circle, legs stretched out in front of them. Charlie Andrews stood in the center of the circle, with a large beach ball. He pivoted slowly, selected a patient at random, and rolled the ball. It bounced into the patient's lap, and he clutched it stupidly. Charlie stepped forward, and traded him a piece of candy for the ball.

"They have a child-like selfishness," Manley said. "As soon as it gets across to Carter that possession of the ball is worth a piece of candy, we'll see a telekinetic in action."

Charlie rolled the ball again. And again. The patients began to register interest, even excitement, as they leaned forward to watch. One patient leaped to his feet to grab the ball, and was ruled out of order. The game continued until each of the thirty-four had received the ball, and won his piece of candy.

"We'll try again tomorrow," Manley said.

They tried again the next day, and the day after that. They kept trying. And on the sixth day the inexplicable happened. The rolling ball suddenly hooked to the left, leaving an eager patient empty-handed while his neighbor claimed the prize. Hollinger and Manley stared, and turned to stare at each other. The winner was not Sidney Carter.

"I'll take over," Manley told Charlie.

He rolled the ball slowly in the same direction. It made the same sharp curve, stopped abruptly, and rolled back across the circle, picking up speed. There was a new winner, also not Sidney Carter. It didn't make sense—or did it?

With trembling fingers, Hollinger got out his notebook and recorded two names.

The patients were bouncing excitedly, rapt enthusiasm on their faces. The ball began to do crazy things. Untouched, it shot back and forth across the circle, swerving to avoid Doctor Manley in the center. The patients' attitude changed to one of strenuous concentration. The ball had a dozen changes of direction before a patient finally seized it and claimed his prize.

Doctor Manley placed the ball in the center of the circle, and walked away. The ball began to roll. From the corner of the room Hollinger followed its wild shifts of direction, and frantically recorded names. The patients were shouting hysterically. The ball came to a complete stop in the center of the circle and remained there, spinning. For a moment, nobody moved.

A patient suddenly scrambled for the ball. Another grabbed his foot and sent him sprawling. And suddenly all the patients were on their feet, screaming, struggling. The ball shot into the air, and stayed there. A bench lifted slowly upwards and hung at a precarious angle. The piano moved a foot out from the wall. Untouched, it slowly began to play a descending scale, from the top of the keyboard. Another scale started at the bottom of the keyboard and moved up rapidly, and both were lost in crashing dissonances. The piano moved another foot.

Manley and Charlie Andrews were waving their arms and shouting orders. Hollinger dropped his notebook into his pocket, and moved out to join them. A little Italian suddenly lifted into the air and plopped onto the hovering bench, his face blank with surprise. The bench dropped away from him and he rose slowly to the ceiling, descended slowly. The piano leaped into the air, and dropped with a splintering thud. Candy erupted from Manley's pocket, and the patients made a reckless, flailing scramble for it.

"We'll need help!" Manley shouted.

Hollinger nodded, and started for the door. A bench hurled past him, turning slowly, end over end, and crashed into the wall. Hollinger suddenly found himself moving backwards, his feet dragging on the linoleum. A polisher whizzed past him on a lightning circuit of the room. Manley and Charlie Andrews stood helplessly among the wildly gesticulating patients, unable to move. The locked door suddenly flew open, and banged against the wall.

The patients made a dash for it, and crowded through. All around the room objects crashed to the floor. Hollinger, Manley and the attendant were suddenly released. Charlie tore into the hallway after the patients, and was propelled back into the room. The door slammed shut. When they tried to open it, they found it locked.

With fumbling fingers Hollinger unlocked the door. The attendant raced down the hallway after the patients. Manley and Hollinger dashed out a side door and across to the administration building. Hollinger stood looking out the window of Manley's office while the Associate Director yelped frantically into a telephone.

The patients of Ward Fifteen were trooping across the lawn, towards the main gate. A guard moved out to intercept them, and ended up perched on a branch of a tree, thirty feet in the air. The gate swung open, and the patients poured out onto the street. A parked car leaped sideways and there was a shrill screech of brakes as a bus crashed into it. The traffic signal in front of the main gate began to swing wildly, snapped loose, and soared in a long arc to crash to the pavement fifty feet away.

The laughing crowd of patients moved across the street to the small business section, and paused in front of a drug store. Candy, cigarettes and assorted merchandise fluttered through the doorway. A pedestrian suddenly found himself hanging two feet off the ground while his feet churned frantically and the contents of his pockets rained onto the sidewalk. The patients scrambled for the coins, and the pedestrian managed to retrieve his wallet and a few other essentials before he fled.

Manley finished his telephoning and joined Hollinger at the window.

"Eighteen," Hollinger said. "I counted eighteen. And there are probably more."

Manley groaned. "Latent telekinetics. All they needed was the proper stimulus, and like damned fools we gave it to them. Now what do we do? We're going to have one hell of a time catching them, and even if we do, we can't put them in a locked room. And I don't suppose a jacket would hold one of them long. We could nail the door shut. Do you suppose they can work nails out of wood? No kind of lock or bolt would keep them in. Maybe we'll have to weld cells for them."

Sirens sounded in the distance. Hospital attendants were racing across the vast grounds towards the main gate. A police car roared up to the curb and an officer leaped out, revolver in hand. He stared stupidly as the revolver soared into the air and stayed there, discharging itself skyward at irregular intervals.

"Once we get this mess straightened out," Manley said, "we're going to do some thorough research. I want to know how those particular men all got into Ward Fifteen. I can't believe it's a coincidence. And I can't believe that telekinesis is something contagious, or . . ."

"Or that *any* insane person has latent *psi* powers?" Hollinger said.

Manley shuddered. More police cars arrived. A fire truck skidded to a halt. The firemen started for a hydrant with their hose, and the hose was seized with convulsions, jerked out of their hands, and slowly ascended vertically into the air. A policeman landed with a thud on the top of his squad car and stretched out there, unable to move. Another unwisely threw a tear gas bomb, and it curved gracefully and went off at his feet.

The office door jerked open, and a nurse hurried in. "Doctor Manley!" she panted.

"What now?" Manley said wearily.

"The oddest thing just happened over in the Women's Division. Ward Thirty-two. A woman was balancing a box on her head, and . . ."

TRAVELING SALESMAN

First published in *Fantastic Universe*, May 1959

The day was Sunday, the time was 5:19 P.M., Eastern Standard Time. Charles Armstrong threw a switch, and stepped through into Time Dimension 7. He experienced nothing but a momentary breathlessness and a slight jolt. The breathlessness he was accustomed to; the jolt irritated him. He moved to his Time Dimension 7 workbench and scribbled on a memo pad, "Raise machine 1/16 inch." Then he hurried up a stairway.

With the aid of a complicated arrangement of peep holes he checked his surroundings carefully before he slid aside a panel and stepped through the wall into a spacious living room. He moved quickly from window to window, looking out at the calm country landscape. A flock of sheep were grazing contentedly just beyond his fence, confident that Armstrong's dogs couldn't get at them. A savage, half-breed dog lay near the fence, watching them hungrily. Far down the hill he could see lights in Farmer Winslow's barn. The farmer would be milking his goats. From the opposite window he looked down on a small, picturesque lake where ducks floated lazily.

Armstrong took out four cartons of dog meat, and went out to feed his dogs. There were four of them, and he had the enclosed space around the cottage fenced into four sections, so the dogs couldn't tear each other apart sometime when he was late in feeding them.

While they gulped their food noisily, he took a rake and carefully circled the dirt path outside his ten-foot fence, smoothing it behind him. He found nothing but a few sheep tracks. Satisfied, he returned to the cottage and dressed himself meticulously.

Impatient to get started, he paced back and forth briefly and finally sat down at his desk, took a copy of H. G. Wells' *The Time*

Machine from a secret compartment and read a few pages into his voicewriter. The machine clicked busily, sliding the finished pages into a pile in front of him. He hesitated several times, looked critically at the voicewritten pages, and read on. When the pile seemed thick enough, he swept the pages into a drawer, concealed the book, and hurried out to his aircar.

The farmer's wife was crossing the yard as he flew over. She waved at him, and he blinked his landing lights in reply. He flew cross-country for ten minutes, turned into the crowded New York air lane, and an hour later set his aircar down on the Times Square landing platform.

He went immediately to a public visiphone, and he self-consciously straightened his tie and tossed his cape back over one shoulder with studied carelessness before he dialed. The screen in front of him shimmered hazily, and abruptly focused.

A girl, blonde, voluptuous and long-limbed, dressed in a semi-transparent lounging robe and very little else, looked out at him expectantly, and squealed with delight.

"Charles, darling, where *have* you been? I've been trying to find you, and nobody knows where that queer country place of yours is."

"Been working," Armstrong said. "Got a couple more chapters done. See you tonight?"

"Sorry, darling. Just impossible—I have too much to do. That's why I wanted to talk to you. I wanted to invite you to my wedding. I'm getting married tomorrow. Now don't carry on so, you darling brute. You look as if you're going to run out and take poison. My getting married doesn't have anything to do with us. I've told you over and over again that I couldn't marry you. The old man wouldn't stand for it."

"I know," Armstrong said. "But I'd hoped . . ."

"Just be reasonable, darling. The old man would disinherit me, and why should I throw away all that money? And Wilber—Wilber Fornis, that's who I'm marrying—he's loaded, too, you know. A girl has to put up with a few inconveniences to be rich. You know yourself it takes years and years for a writer to make any money, and you'll never get rich as long as you write those queer stories. Now don't let it bother you—there's a boy. Give me a call in about a month, and we'll arrange a nice weekend together. I'll cheer you up!"

"I don't know," Armstrong said slowly. "Anyway—I wish you all kinds of happiness."

She stared at him. "Now that's a hell of a thing to say to someone who's getting married. What's the matter with you, anyway?"

Armstrong half-promised to call her in a month, and cut off. He kicked the wall of the visiphone booth savagely. "What a damnable beginning! This trip will probably be another flop." He studied his appearance in the mirror, straightened his tie again, and dialed another number.

This girl was a brunette, demure and not especially attractive. She stared at him, clapped her hand to her mouth, and glanced behind her cautiously. "Charles! You weren't supposed to call me again!"

Armstrong's pent-up irritation exploded. "I can't help it, damn it! Do you love me, or don't you?"

She faltered. "Yes. I—I love you. But dad forbade me to see you again. He said you're just a fortune hunter. He says he'll change his will if I marry you. He'll even change it if I don't stop seeing you."

Armstrong grinned, confident again. Fathers always came around, eventually. All it took was a grandchild. "Let him change it," he said. "We don't need his money. I don't even want it. We can get along if we love each other, can't we?"

"Oh, yes, I suppose we could. But I'd hate to make Dad and Moms unhappy. It's not just your being a writer, but if only you'd write something *respectable*."

"I will," Armstrong said fervently. "I'll forget all about the science fiction. What do you want me to write?"

"No." She shook her head sadly. "No. You must be true to yourself. I know you'll be a great writer, some day, and I'll always be proud that I've known you. But please don't call me again."

Abruptly the screen went blank. Armstrong swore violently, and slammed the door after him as he left the booth. He'd botched things up nicely.

He walked down West Forty-Second Street to a small, crumbly hotel, mounted to the second floor, and knocked on the door. Two knocks, a pause, then three knocks. The door opened a crack,

Armstrong was cautiously scrutinized and admitted, and the door was quickly closed behind him. A wizened scarecrow of a man peered at Armstrong through thick glasses. "Got any?"

Armstrong took a bottle of aspirin tablets from his pocket, and placed it on the table. Trembling fingers seized the bottle, dumped the contents onto a dirty piece of paper, and counted deftly. "Hundred—got any more?"

Armstrong produced another bottle. It was dumped, and the contents quickly counted. The man took one tablet from each bottle, and tasted carefully. "Good stuff. Got any more?"

"Not this trip."

He nodded, took a thick roll of bills from his pocket, and reluctantly counted the money into Armstrong's hand. One thousand, two thousand credits.

Armstrong scowled. "Price gone down?"

"Has to. Feds are really getting tough. Costs a hell of a lot to distribute the stuff. Might lose money on this batch. I'm getting out of New York, in a couple of days, until things quiet down."

"I'm thinking of switching to Philadelphia," Armstrong said. "Got any connections there?"

"Yeah—Philly. Might go to Philly myself. When'll you have some more stuff?"

"Hard to say."

"There's a little frozen foods store way out on Market Street. Marty's Frozen Foods. When you get some stuff, you ask Marty how to get hold of Chip. I'll leave word."

"Will do," Armstrong said.

He hurried out of the hotel and walked back towards Times Square, glancing furtively over his shoulder to see if he was being followed. He entered a restaurant, found an empty booth, and dialed his order. He leaned back thoughtfully while he waited.

It was a hell of a mess, he thought. No matter how hard he worked, nothing seemed to work out. He hadn't had any success for a year and a half—anywhere—and now there wasn't one grade A businessman left in the entire New York area that he could consider a prospective father-in-law. He'd either have to shift his base of operations, or pull out.

But he didn't want to pull out. He liked Time Dimension 7. It was as good a place to live as any Time Dimension he'd found.

He'd have to start over again in Philadelphia. He could still be a writer, but he wouldn't write science fiction. That had been a serious mistake, but of course, he hadn't known that when he started out. He'd thought a Time Dimension as scientifically advanced as No. 7 would be enthused about science fiction. But they seemed to like old-fashioned stuff. Dickens—he wondered if they would like Dickens. He'd have to edit the stuff, which would be a lot of work, but with a voicewriter it should be possible. He could do a little study, and make himself a writer of historical novels. Hell—Dickens was supposed to be a good writer. His stuff *should* be successful. The next time he got back to Time Dimension 1 he'd pick up the complete works of Dickens.

He finished his meal and walked back to the parking platform, where he entered a visiphone booth and placed a mail subscription for three months of Philadelphia newspapers. The society pages would be a good place to start looking for eligible heiresses, and when he got a list made up he could start checking on their fathers.

He flew back to his cottage without incident. It was 22:30 Eastern Standard Time in Time Dimension 7, and the farmhouse was dark. Armstrong climbed into his Time Dimension 7 bed, and had himself gently rocked asleep.

The bed awakened him at seven, by rocking gently, then firmly, and finally dumping him onto the floor when he failed to respond. He placed a frozen breakfast unit on the stove to heat while he was dressing. After eating, he stepped through the wall panel to the concealed stairway, and descended to his basement workroom. For the next hour he methodically visited each of the eleven Time Dimensions in which he had a base established, fed his dogs, and carefully inspected the ground outside each fence for signs of intruders.

His last stop was time Dimension 3. There, in one end of his cottage living room, he had a machine shop, with a stationary stream engine furnishing power from a shed outside. On his work bench was a small gasoline engine, the product of Time Dimension 1. Armstrong had disassembled it, made a scale drawing of each part, carefully removed all identifying marks of the manufacturer, and reassembled it. He could have built one himself, but it seemed a waste of time when he could acquire one ready-made.

He changed into a costume suitable for Time dimension 3, and busied himself with building a crate for the gasoline engine. It was nearly ten o'clock when he finished. He strolled down the hill to the farmhouse, and found Farmer Hilton waiting for him with a horse and buggy.

The farmer grinned happily as his rough hand crushed Armstrong's.

"Saw ya comin', so I hitched her up," he said.

"Well, now, that was nice of you. Anything I can bring you from town?"

"Oh, no—you been too good to us, Mr. Armstrong. Glad to help you out."

Armstrong nodded his thanks, and drove the buggy back up to the cottage. He loaded in the gasoline engine, and carefully padlocked the gate after him as he drove away. The padlock he had made himself—copying the best lock he could buy in Time Dimension 1.

Armstrong drove into Princeton on tortuously muddy roads, left his horse and buggy at a livery stable, and caught the train to Newark, taking the gasoline into the coach with him as hand baggage. At Newark, he hired a horse and buggy, loaded in his gasoline engine, and drove out into the country to the estate of his Time Dimension 3 father-in-law.

He drove up the broad, horseshoe shaped drive to the sprawling house, and his wife Victoria burst joyously from the veranda and threw herself into his arms. "Was the train late, darling? I'm so glad you didn't get lost in your work and forget to come. Daddy has some kind of important meeting for you tonight, and it would have disappointed him terribly. Charlie, Charlie, see who's here!"

Charles Armstrong, Jr., toddled down the steps, his two-year-old face puckered into an impish grin. He gave his father a rough but respectful hug, searching in his pockets for candy, found some, and munched cheerfully. Time Dimension 3 candy. In a moment of carelessness Armstrong had once brought home some delicacies from Time Dimension 1, and caused a sensation. For months afterwards the entire household had been after him to buy more. But it was, he explained, something that had to be imported, and he hadn't been able to find any.

Armstrong arranged with a stable boy to return his rented horse and buggy, and tenderly carried the gasoline engine up onto the veranda. Victoria looked at it wide-eyed. "You've finished it? Oh, Charles!"

His mother-in-law regarded it sedately. She was no more than forty-five, but she was the sedate kind of woman, and Time Dimension 3 was a sedate civilization. "Roger will be pleased," she said. "It's hard to convince men they should invest money in something they haven't seen. But if it works—it does work, doesn't it?"

"Mother!" Victoria exclaimed. "Of course, it works. Didn't my husband build it?"

Mrs. Cahill smiled faintly, and returned to her knitting.

"We'll have a demonstration when dad gets home," Armstrong said. "You'll find that it's an infernally noisy thing, but it works very well."

"Do you have to go back tomorrow?" Victoria asked anxiously.

"I'm afraid so. Still have lots of work to do on this."

"I'd hoped we could take a lunch and have a picnic—just the three of us."

"Too muddy," Mrs. Cahill said firmly. "Not good for Victoria anyway."

"Oh, Mother!"

"Don't tell me you haven't told him."

"But Mother . . ."

"A husband's got a right to know. A *duty* to know. After all . . ."

Armstrong stared at Victoria's blushing face. "What's all this? You don't mean to say—that's wonderful!"

"I'm so happy, Charles," she whispered. "And Charlie needs a little brother or sister. Are you happy? Oh, Charles!"

She flung herself into his arms, and Mrs. Cahill dryly collected her knitting and left.

That evening the family and a half-dozen businessmen that Cahill had invited in sat in a circle watching Armstrong's gasoline engine pound away, noisily. Mrs. Cahill and Victoria held their hands over their ears and grimaced painfully. Charles, Junior, watched open-mouthed and the eyes of the businessmen were glistening dollar signs.

Later, they retired to the house, and the men gathered in Roger Cahill's study for what Armstrong regarded as a painful two hours of business chatter. The men left, eventually, and Cahill pressed another cigar on Armstrong, had a new supply of drinks brought in, and leaned back contentedly.

"I don't doubt," he said, "that this engine will be everything you say it will. And it will make a fortune for both of us. We'll own fifty-two per cent of the stock between us, and you'll be getting a nice royalty on every engine the company makes. Then there'll be those other ideas of yours—that lock, for one thing. That should cause a sensation. I give you just five years to make your first million. The second million will come quicker, of course."

"I'm afraid I'm not very practical in business matters," Armstrong said, "Without you to back me, I probably couldn't have brought this off."

"Nonsense. You'd have made out all right."

"Just the same, I'm glad to have someone I can trust to manage things for me. You look after the fussiness end of it, and let me do the inventing. I'm sure it'll work out best that way."

Cahill nodded. He did not look dissatisfied. "I'm rather happy the way things have worked out," he said. "I don't mind saying I had my doubts about you, at first. Thought you were one of these blasted fortune hunters, and I was certain your marriage to Vicky wouldn't last a year. But you've made her as happy as any girl could be. She'd like to have you around more, of course, but I know how much sweat goes into something like this, and I'm sure she understands."

"I hope this goes all right," Armstrong said. "After all that work on the electric light . . ."

"Don't let that worry you. They're interested, all right. I'll have the money in the morning. And when we're big enough, we can get to work on that electric light again. We've got the patents, so there's nothing to worry about. There wasn't anything wrong with the idea. It just took more capital than I could swing."

Armstrong nodded. The electric light was his first Time Dimension 3 invention, but he ran into stubborn resistance. After all, what was wrong with gas? Why spend all that money for a powerplant and transmission lines when people were happy the way things were. And wasn't electricity dangerous? Even his father-in-law had been skeptical. But the gasoline engine seemed to be going over. Now he was toying with the idea of inventing the telegraph.

Perhaps he could get the government interested in financing a trial installation.

Victoria was waiting for Armstrong in their bedroom. "You're getting too important," she said. "Now I can't even have you when you get home."

It was early the next afternoon when Armstrong drove his buggy up to the Hilton Farm. The Hiltons' ten year old son took charge of the horse, and also the package of presents Armstrong had bought for the family in Newark. Armstrong felt a warm affection for the Hiltons. He wished he could do something for them. Something big. Whenever he saw sturdy, red-faced, kindly Mrs. Hilton laboring in the barn his conscience bothered him. He wanted to give them a milking machine, but there were just too many complications. He would have to go slow—he'd learned that much. It wouldn't do to spring something that involved half a dozen complicated inventions.

But once he got the gasoline engine on the market, perhaps he could manage it. He could develop a milking machine powered by the gasoline engine. He could, that is, if some essential material wasn't lacking in the Time Dimension 3 economy. He'd have to check on that.

He looked his cottage over carefully, fed his dogs, and then visited the other ten Time Dimensions. He fed his dogs, inspected the automatic feeders he'd set up for the times when he might have to be absent a few days, checked for prowlers, and allowed himself to be seen by the farmer in each Time Dimension. In Time Dimension 7 he walked down to the farmhouse and picked up his mail—the accumulations of newspapers from Philadelphia.

Satisfied that everything was in order, he stepped through into Time Dimension 19. His cottage was a glistening, pre-fabricated structure of an aluminum alloy, and there was a sleek atomic-powered automobile in his garage. Armstrong drove to Princeton on a broad, smoothly surfaced highway. He stopped to make two phone calls, and drove on to New York.

His first stop was the office of a stout industrialist. That worthy gentleman pawed eagerly at the small bag of cheap industrial diamonds that Armstrong gave him. He spread them out on his desk, beamed happily at them, weighed them carefully, and counted out an impressive pile of cash for Armstrong.

Armstrong could buy industrial diamonds for next to nothing in Time Dimension 3, where industry was still in its infancy. And a few of these same diamonds brought a gratifying price in highly industrialized Time Dimension 19, where the demand was incessant—and where the diamonds of Central and South Africa had never been discovered.

Armstrong's second stop was the home of a charming young debutant. Armstrong took her to dinner, made bright conversation with her, and very correctly and properly took her home. Society in Time Dimension 19 was organized along very correct and proper lines. Armstrong had been engaged to a lovely young heiress, and two weeks before their wedding date, she had gotten herself tragically killed in an automobile accident. It was another of Armstrong's long series of frustrations.

But he had to conduct himself correctly and properly about the whole thing. He had retired for a suitable period of mourning, and now he was gradually easing himself back into circulation. There were enough heiresses among the friends of his former fiancée to provide a wide field of selection. The only question was, which father would make the most desirable father-in-law? Armstrong was uncertain, but he was studying the problem carefully. When he made up his mind, he would pick a suitable profession to match his father-in-law's talent. In the meantime, he was doing very well with the diamonds.

Armstrong checked into a hotel for the night, and in the morning he drove back to his cottage, made his usual inspection tour, and stepped through into Time Dimension 5. He flew his helicopter in to Princeton, made a half-dozen telephone calls, found a half-dozen young ladies unavailable, unenthused, or under paternal edict, and flew angrily back to his cottage. He couldn't see any break at all in the bad luck that had plagued him for a year and a half.

In Time Dimension 12 he sat down in front of a typewriter, and worked busily at copying Hemingway's *The Old Man and the Sea*. He thought Hemingway would make a highly successful writer in Time Dimension 12. The problem was in editing the background of a story. He couldn't use *For whom the Bell Tolls*, because a war about the Spanish Revolution wouldn't make much sense in a Time Dimension where there hadn't been any Spanish Revolution.

And *A Farewell to Arms* set in World War I Italy created some problems in a Time Dimension where Italy had not participated in World War I. Both novels could be adapted to other settings, but that would take work, so he was starting out with *The Old Man and the Sea*.

He worked industriously for three hours. Then he collected the pages he had typed, got out his automobile, and drove to New York. It was a normal automobile, much like those of Time Dimension 1, but less streamlined, and with less chrome, fewer gadgets, and much, much better performance. The engineers in Time Dimension 12 were more concerned about what a car did than how it looked. In most respects, though, Time Dimension 12 was startlingly similar to Time Dimension 1. It was the most normal world that Armstrong had discovered.

It was evening when Armstrong reached the Long Island home of his wife's parents. His wife, a chubby but not unattractive blonde girl, greeted him affectionately, and hauled him off to the nursery to view the latest antics of Charles Armstrong, Jr. The plump six-month-old baby gurgled and cooed and displayed exhibitionistic tendencies to delight the proudest parents.

It wasn't until later, when she had Armstrong settled comfortably on a sofa and herself settled comfortably on his lap, that she asked him how the book was coming.

"Wonderful," Armstrong said. "I'm really breezing along. I should have it finished in a couple of weeks."

"Dad will be happy to hear that."

"He will?" Armstrong said doubtfully.

"He will now. He took what you have finished over to a professor friend of his and the professor says you're an out and out genius. Entirely new style, and all that. It'll revolutionize modern American letters. Dad is so pleased to have a genius in the family that he's going to publish it no matter what his editors say."

"I really don't think he should," Armstrong said seriously. "I can always find my own publisher, and if his firm isn't sold on the book . . ."

"Don't be silly. What's the point in having a publisher for a father-in-law if you don't let him publish your book?"

"I'll have to talk to him about it," Armstrong said.

"He'll convince you. He's all enthused, now. And he's the boss, so it really doesn't matter what his editors say. He'd be tickled pink to have it become a best seller after they told him not to publish it."

"I hardly think . . ."

She interrupted him with a kiss. "Oh, don't be so modest. How about flying down to Florida for a couple of days?"

Armstrong hesitated. He hated to waste time. But then—this trip was building up to another total loss, and some relaxation might be good for him. "Sure," he said. "A little time away from the book might be healthy for me. When do we leave?"

Armstrong was back at his cottage Tuesday morning. He made his usual round of inspection, and stopped off for a brief check on Time Dimension 10. World War II wasn't over yet, in Time Dimension 10, though the end was expected almost any day. Armstrong was keeping discreetly out of sight. He didn't want to get into difficulties as a draft dodger, and he felt that he'd done his share of fighting World War II in Time Dimension 1.

During the afternoon he was in to Princeton four times and back again, in Time Dimension 5, 9, 11, and 16, and he scored no progress. Worse than no progress. He had the definite feeling that he was losing ground. Some of the damned fathers of girls on his lists infuriated him. They thought he was after their money, and a father-in-law's money was the last thing Armstrong yearned for. What he wanted, what he had to have, was a good business manager in every Time Dimension. A father-in-law made an ideal business manager, if he was a good business man. He could be trusted. He could do all right for himself, too.

But these thundering idiots called him a fortune hunter, and accused him of wanting to marry their daughters for their money.

By the time he reached Time Dimension 14, Armstrong was in a seething, sputtering rage. He stomped about the room, smashing test tubes on the floor. "Get it over with," he told himself. "Wind this up in a hurry, and go home. Next trip you can make a clean start. You've wasted enough time. No results for a year and a half . . ."

He stalked down to the farmhouse, and got his horse and buggy.

Time Dimension 14 was a horse-and-buggy civilization, but the automobile was coming into use, electric lights, the telegraph and telephone had already been invented, and with the most obvious inventions already spoken for, Armstrong had gone into another field. His decision had been influenced by the fact that he had a prosperous drug manufacturer as a prospective father-in-law—but that wasn't working out, either. When the situation had looked more hopeful, Armstrong had set himself up as a scientist, and given himself a thorough course in general research chemistry and bacteriology.

Evening found Armstrong calling at a sprawling monstrosity of a house in Trenton. The girl was very glad to see him, and very frightened about his being there. Armstrong, in his eagerness to wind things up, used a brusque frontal attack that terrified her.

"Do you love me, or don't you?" he snapped.

"Charles! You know . . ."

"I know nothing of the kind. I don't care what your father thinks of me. I'm not marrying *him*. You're of age, and you're old enough to make up your own mind. Either we get married tomorrow, or you'll never see me again. Which will it be?"

She stood before him and sobbed convulsively. She was a small girl, plain-looking, with an overly-large nose that completely spoiled her face. But he suspected that underneath the layers of clothing that females wore in this Time Dimension she might have an enticingly arranged figure.

He watched her coldly until she lifted her tear-stained face, and whispered, "I'll marry you."

Electrified, he seized her in his arms and danced about the room.

"Father," she whispered. "What will I tell Father?"

"Let me talk to your father," Armstrong said confidently.

Ebenezer White did not greet Armstrong joyfully. He was a robust, middle-aged man with prematurely white hair, and the sight of Armstrong fired his naturally pink complexion into a flaming red. "I've told you sir," he thundered, "that you are not welcome in my house."

"Your daughter and I are getting married tomorrow," Armstrong said coolly. "If possible, with your blessings. If necessary, without."

White sputtered impotently, and his red face took on a definite tinge of purple. "I see. I suppose there's nothing I can do about *that*. But I'll have you know, you scamp, that you'll never lay a hand on my money or business.

"If that's all that's bothering you," Armstrong said, "why don't you call a lawyer now, and make the necessary arrangements? I have enough money for us to live on comfortably, and every expectation of future success. But frankly, I think it would be best for Janis to live here with you. I spend a lot of time at my laboratory, and she wouldn't like being alone. For her sake, I think we should be able to work out some reasonable arrangement."

There was skepticism in White's wry smile. "Do you actually mean you have no objection to my putting my estate in trust for Janis? You wouldn't be able to touch it, you know, and the executor would keep a careful watch on what she did with her money."

"Sounds like a sensible arrangement," Armstrong said. "I'm certainly no businessman—I'm a scientist. I couldn't blame you in the least for wanting your estate in capable hands."

White stared at Armstrong. "I don't quite understand this. My daughter is no raving beauty. Frankly, I consider her homely. And you're a handsome man. Why would you want to marry my daughter, if not for her money?"

"Perhaps Janis told you, sir, that I've been married before. I married my first wife because she was beautiful. It's a rare woman who can be beautiful and stay that way. I vowed that if I ever married again, I'd look for other qualities than beauty."

"I see," White said. He fumbled in a drawer, found a lavishly polished corncob pipe, and got it lit. "Your—ah—work. Have you found a cure for smallpox yet? " He chuckled.

"Not a cure, sir. A *prevention*. Yes, I believe I've found it."

White dropped his pipe, and stared. "You have?"

"Yes, sir. All I need is the right firm to produce and sell it."

White's face was almost back to its normal pink. His eyes narrowed. "Seems to me there'd be quite a market for something like that. Every man, woman and child in America would be a potential customer."

"Every man, woman and child in the world, sir."

"In the world," White repeated. "Every man, woman and child in the world." His eyes gleamed brightly. "I'd like to talk to you about that—after the honeymoon, of course."

"After the honeymoon," Armstrong agreed. They shook hands.

Nine days later Armstrong drove up in front of his Time Dimension 1 apartment house, and began unloading packages from his car. From an upstairs window Mrs. Hallihan looked down, nudged Mrs. Hones, who was a new tenant, and said, "There he is—that's Armstrong. He's late this trip. Handsome brute, isn't he?" I always said a woman's a fool to marry a good-looking man like that, and let him be a traveling salesman. We used to say he dealt exclusively in lingerie, and we didn't mean selling it, either. Once when he was supposed to be out on the road I saw him myself, coming out of that big apartment building down the street with a woman that lived there. There was a woman right here in this building, too—and him with six children, and his wife used to be such a pretty thing. Never could figure out why he wanted to be a salesman. Not the type, you know. We always said he couldn't sell hot soup to the Eskimos. What he really ought to be is a mechanic, or something like that. He can fix anything, TV sets, and radios, and cars—real handy with his hands. You should see some of the things he's built. But he had to be a traveling salesman—wanted to get out so he could chase women, I suppose. His family had a terrible time, and he lost one job after another because he wouldn't work and they were always about to be evicted. But the last three years or so he's settled down and tended to business. He's been making plenty of money, and they moved down to a first-floor apartment and got all new furniture, and you should see the new television set they bought last month. I couldn't say—maybe he just got too old for it. Men get that way, you know, though he certainly doesn't *look* it..."

Armstrong looked up, and saw the faces in the upstairs window. That nosey Mrs. Hallihan, and the other would be the new tenant who was just moving in when he left. Bah! He really should get out of this dumpy apartment, and buy a house somewhere. But it wouldn't do to get prosperous *too* quickly.

The Armstrong family poured out of the front door. The five girls jumped up and down excitedly on the porch, and five-year-old Charles, Junior, tore down the steps and hurled himself at his father.

"Bring me something this time, Daddy?"

"Sure," Armstrong said. "Lots of presents for everyone."

Mrs. Armstrong greeted her husband with a motherly kiss on the cheek.

"Sorry I'm late," Armstrong said. "Had to make a side trip to Chicago."

"Quite all right, darling. Have a nice trip? How was business?"

"Not bad, my dear," Armstrong said, beaming. "Not bad at all. I landed a new account."

ESIDARAP OT PIRT DNUOR

First published in *If Science Fiction*, November 1960

Jeff Allen pressed his nose against the door and steamed the glass with an angry snort. "A bomb would do it," he said. "Something big enough to make a nice bang and clean out the office, but not big enough to knock over the building. Ann, where can we get a bomb?"

His wife looked up from her typewriter and smiled. "Don't be ridiculous. You're getting all riled up over nothing."

Allen whirled and stomped over to the counter. "Nothing, you call it? You know very well that Centralia is just not big enough to support *two* travel agencies. We were doing pretty well, but cut our business in half and we'll starve to death."

"Business hasn't fallen off since he opened up. In fact, it's improved."

"Ann, you know that's a temporary fluke. It's bound to fall off. Any business he does has to cut into our business. There's no other place for it to come from. So where can I get a bomb?"

She laughed, and he leaned over to kiss her before he went gloomily back to his desk. Things had probably been going too smoothly, he told himself, what with the boom brought on by the travel-now-pay-later plans. He was just fifteen hundred dollars short of a down payment on that rambling California redwood ten-room ranch house with a rustic lake view, and he and Ann had been working and planning ever since their marriage three years before—working hard—to build the business to a point where she could retire from her role as clerk and personal secretary and concentrate on being a housewife with perhaps a robust crop of little Allens.

And now the whole picture was wrecked by a villainous-looking man with a brownish-red beard and a spectacularly bald head, who had appeared suddenly in Centralia and opened a new travel agency directly across the street from Allen's Globe Travel Agency. And he'd had the infernal nerve to name his business the Gloob Travel Agency.

"What did the Chamber of Commerce say?" Ann asked.

"They're puzzled," said Allen. "Gloob seems to be an obvious infringement on Globe. On the other hand, he says his name is Gloob, so how can we keep him from using his own name? They're going to investigate. And I stopped by for a brief conversation with Mr. Gloob. He was deliriously happy to meet me and certain we will get along fine together. He even promised to send me any business he can't handle himself, which convinces me that he has a fiendish sense of humor." He shook his head. "I suppose we might as well let Doris go—give her notice, anyway."

"But business hasn't fallen off. Let's wait and see what happens. There'll be plenty of time...."

A tiny, gray-haired old lady pushed open the door and stepped briskly to the counter. "I wish immediate accommodations for Sirap," she said.

Ann frowned. "For—what was the place?"

"Sirap."

"What country is that in?"

The old lady cocked her head to one side and cast puzzled glances about the office. "Oh, I'm sorry!" she said suddenly. "I must have the wrong..."

She stepped briskly out and the door whipped shut behind her, cutting off the blast of warm air from the street.

Ann's golden head bent studiously over an atlas. "There's a Siret in Romania," she said. "But it's a river."

"I thought there was something fishy about her," Allen said.

He went to the window and watched her cross the street and walk confidently into the Gloob Travel Agency. She did not emerge, but as he watched, a portly gentleman came out and crossed the street to the Globe Travel Agency. He paused inside the door, sniffed deeply at the air conditioning and gave a deep sigh of appreciation.

"Feels good in here," he announced. He walked to the counter and smiled down at Ann. "I'd like to arrange an extended tour of the United States. Could you handle it for me?"

Ann caught her breath. "Yes, *sir*."

"This is what I'd like to do. Start out with a week in Detroit and then go to Cleveland...."

His voice rumbled on and Ann took notes feverishly. "It will take a little time to arrange this," she said. "Where can we reach you?"

"At the Centralia Hotel."

"All right, Mr.—"

"Smith. John Smith."

"Mr. Smith. We'll get to work on it immediately."

"Excuse me," Allen said, "but didn't I see you coming out of the Gloob Travel Agency?"

The gentleman turned and beamed at him. "Indeed you did. The man there recommended you."

Allen returned to his desk, leaned back in his chair, and gnawed fretfully on a pencil.

There was a brawny, bald-headed man who drawled with a foreign-sounding accent and seemed nervously anxious to get to Nilreb with much haste. There was a sedate, middle-aged woman who hovered in the background while two teen-aged girls inquired with assorted giggles, as to whether Dnalsi Yenoc was actually anywhere near Kroywen, and whether they could go direct, or by way of Nylkoorb. And there were others.

Eventually Ann stopped fumbling with the atlas, and in time she even grew weary of explanations. She contented herself with pointing, and when people with odd destinations sighted along her wavering finger and glimpsed Mr. Gloob's sign, they invariably bounded away with unconcealed enthusiasm.

In between these visitations, the Globe Travel Agency's business boomed past all rational proportions. Allen made the down payment on the ranch house, and when Ann insisted that they were too busy for her to consider taking up housekeeping, he hired two new office girls. And the boom continued.

"Have you noticed," he said to Ann two weeks later, "that more than eighty per cent of our customers are not residents of Centralia?"

"I've been wondering about that," she said.

"And have you noticed that we're getting fewer inquiries from people with cockeyed destinations?"

"There was only one yesterday," Ann said, "and not any today."

She paused as a white-haired, scholarly-looking man stopped on the sidewalk outside, scrutinized them doubtfully through the window, and finally entered to ask to reservations to Kroywen. Ann pointed at the Gloob sign and he left, muttering apologies.

"Kroywen," Allen mused, "I've heard that one before,"

"Same here," said Ann.

"I've got to get to the bottom of this. Mr. Gloob goes out to lunch at twelve-thirty. About a quarter to one I'm going over to the Gloob Travel Agency and see if I can arrange a fast trip to Kroywen."

"Not without me, you aren't," Ann said.

T hey left the mystified Doris with instructions to carry on if they should be delayed, bank the money and sign any necessary checks with a limited power of attorney. They marched across Main Street, invaded the Gloob Travel Agency, and were met by Mr. Gloob's smiling assistant.

"Kroywen," Allen said, "Make it snappy."

"Two for Kroywen," the young man said complacently. "That will be sixty-two dollars and fifty cents."

Allen counted it out.

"Do you have any money to exchange?"

"Why—ah—no," Allen said.

"No luggage?"

"No. You see…"

"I quite understand. It's best that way. Now if you will receipt these papers…"

With one deft motion he took Allen's right hand, inked his thumb, rolled a print onto the paper and wiped the thumb clean. "And yours, please," he said to Ann. "Thank you. Have a nice tour."

"Thank you,"

"You may find the people a bit backward."

Allen said cheerfully, "We don't mind."

"Most people don't. Right this way, please."

They followed him through a rear door, rode an escalator down to the basement, and paused in front of a metal bulge in the wall. He opened it.

"Be seated, please," he said. "Remain seated until the door opens."

After they sat down, he smiled and told them to come again. The door closed. They were in a tubelike chamber which had six rows of seats dipping across the curved floor.

"It's like a carnival," Ann said, "Twenty-five cents for a tour of the Chamber of Horrors. Or maybe it's a subway car."

"Yeah. But what is it doing in Centralia, Ohio? I wonder if the Interstate Commerce Commission knows about this."

There was a jerk, so insignificant that they would not have noticed it had they not been tensed in anticipation of – something. A light flashed red and faded slowly. They looked blankly at each other as the door opened. Another young man was peering in at them.

"Some ride," Allen growled.

"Destination," the young man said, "Kroywen terminal. All out please."

They stepped out and followed him.

"Right this way to Customs," he said.

They paused at a desk marked "Customs" and a young lady noted their lack of baggage, glanced in a cursory manner at the contents of Ann's purse and waved them past. They walked out into what was obviously the concourse of a transportation terminal. There were ticket windows, travelers wandering about with bags, and a large schedule, listing arrivals and departures from and to tongue-twisting places. Allen looked back at the door they had just emerged from, and saw a large sign.

BOOLG INCORPORATED
Specialists in Travel Curiosities

"That's no lie," he said.

They settled themselves on uncomfortable seats at the far end of the concourse and looked around. Allen stared at a clock.

"Screwy time they have here," he said, "That clock says five after eleven. My watch says five to one. How about yours?"

"Five to one," Ann said.

"What should we do? I guess we've proved there's such a place as Kroywen. Shall we go back?"

"It might look funny if we went back right away."

"True. So we've proved there is a Kroywen, but where is it? I'd like to know...What's the matter?"

Ann's elbow had dug sharply at his ribs. "The second hand on that clock is running backwards," she said.

Allen studied it, "So is the minute hand." And a few minutes later, "So is the hour hand."

Ann looked at her watch. "Then when we have one o'clock, they have eleven o'clock. And when we have..."

"Two, they have ten. And so on. It's just like our time, only in reverse."

Ann was studying the Boolg, Incorporated, sign. "Boolg," she said. "Now if you spell that backwards..."

Allen did so, mouthing it slowly. He turned to Ann. "Gloob! The Gloob Travel Agency!"

"And this town. Kroywen. Could that be..."

"New York!"

"It must be."

"It's somebody's idea of a joke."

"We're here, aren't we?"

"But *where* are we?" Allen said. "Something like twenty seconds from Centralia, and New York is nearly six hundred miles. And which way did we go? East, or west, or straight down?"

"I was just thinking of something Gloob's assistant said. Remember? He said we may find the people a bit backward."

Allen shrugged. "Shall we take a quick look at the town?"

"We might as well. I've never been to New York."

"You *still* haven't been to New York."

They rode an escalator up three stories and found an exit. A uniformed man called out, "Taxi?" as they went out the door.

"They speak English," Allen said.

"And not in reverse," said Ann. "That's a blessing."

The street was a brightly illuminated tunnel, with a high, arching ceiling. There were throngs of people on the walks, and throngs of vehicles in the street.

"The underside," Ann said. "Maybe like reflections in the water. Maybe somewhere straight up is the real New York."

Allen had stopped to watch passengers boarding a bus.

"We can't take it," Ann said, "You didn't get any money changed."

"How was I to know what we'd find here? Anyway, I was just looking. The traffic moves on the left side and the bus drivers sit in the rear. How can they see where they're going?"

"Maybe they have front-view mirrors."

They turned away as the bus rumbled off. They walked for what seemed to be miles along the tunneled streets, wandering about aimlessly, spelling the names of buildings and places and streets backwards, and finding some that they recognized. They found Broadway and Fifth Avenue, and the Etats Eripme Building, the deepest building in the world. They resisted the temptation to visit its observations gallery, remembering at the last moment, that they had no money.

"It's just another big city," Ann said. "Too many people, and too crowded, and too much noise."

"And no blue sky," Allen said, "They must have some sky somewhere. Where do you suppose they keep it?"

When they next thought about the time it was after five—or before seven, Kroywen time. And they were definitely ready to leave. They found their way back to the terminal and rode the escalator down to the concourse. Ann turned suddenly and clutched Allen's arm. "How are you going to buy tickets?"

"I've got plenty of money."

"Dollars. But you didn't get any money changed. What if they won't take dollars?"

"Anyone will take dollars. They took dollars at the other end, didn't they? And if they won't there should be somewhere we can get them changed."

"I hope you're right," Ann said. "Thinking backwards is all right for one afternoon, but I'm too old to do it permanently."

Allen grinned down at the young face she called old, and they walked hand in hand across the concourse to Boolg, Incorporated. At the door they stopped in consternation. Boolg, Incorporated, was closed. "Hours 3 to 7" read the sign on the door.

"Well!" Ann said.

Allen counted on his fingers. "Which means nine to five. My watch says five-twenty."

"So what do we do now?" asked Ann. "Sit in the station all night?"

"Certainly not. We'll go to a hotel."

"How are you going to pay the hotel bill?"

"I can get some money changed in the morning."

"All right," she said.

They advanced self-consciously to the registration desk of the Reltats Hotel and faced the suspicious scrutiny of the room clerk. He looked them over, noted their lack of luggage, and said with a sneer, "Married, no doubt?"

Allen spoke indignantly. "Of course we're married. We've been married for three years."

He was not prepared for the clerk's reaction. The man's face reddened and he sputtered and waved his hands menacingly. Two more clerks came to his aid. The first clerk pointed a finger at them. "Married!" he blurted out.

"You mean they *admit* it?"

"The idea—at a first-class hotel, too. What do they think we are?"

"Call the police."

Allen grabbed Ann's arm and ran. Outside the door a bellhop caught up with them, scribbled something on a piece of paper and handed it to Allen.

"Try this place," he said. "It isn't a bad hotel and they aren't so particular. But it'd be best not to tell them you're married. It doesn't matter what they think, but when you come right out and say it..."

"Thanks," Allen said.

"Don't mention it fellow. I was married once myself."

The hotel was small, clean, and almost primly respectable in atmosphere. The room clerk snickered when Allen signed the register, but said nothing. Allen told him they would be staying one night, and fifteen rallods seemed a proper price, and the clerk turned them over to a cheery-looking bellhop. They entered an elevator and dropped.

"It seems all right," Ann whispered. "What's the matter?"

"I'm trying to figure out how to tip the bellhop."

That worthy escorted them to their room, took a quick turn-around it to see that everything was in order, and as Allen self-consciously turned his back to him, he thrust something into Allen's hand on the way out.

"Of all the insults!" Allen exploded as the door closed. "I didn't make any move to tip him, so *he* tipped *me* three rollods!"

Ann took one of the bills. "Pretty good picture of Notgnihsaw," she said. "Do you think this would buy us a meal?"

"Probably not—not a good meal, anyway. And I'm hungry. We could have something sent up and put it on our bill. Maybe there's a menu around here somewhere."

Their food arrived, accompanied by the same grinning bellhop. Allen cringed in embarrassment at the thought of offering the man his own three rallods as a tip, but the bellhop gave him no opportunity. He deftly slipped some currency onto one tray and hurried out.

"He tipped me again!" Allen yelped. "This time it's five rallods?"

"Don't complain," Ann said. "Maybe we can work up enough to pay our hotel bill."
"Nothing doing. Here, I'll put it all on the tray. The least I can do is offer him his money back."

When the bellhop came for the trays, he carefully removed the money and placed it on the desk. And when Allen picked it up later, there were no longer eight rallods, but eleven.

The day had been exhausting and they slept well. It was after nine when they awoke—not quite three, Kroywen time—and they ate breakfast in the hotel dining room to avoid further insults from the bellhop, having the check transferred to their hotel bill. Then Ann returned to their room, and Allen strolled down to the terminal to exchange some money and arrange their return to Centralia.

The young man at Boolg, Incorporated, was sympathetic. "The rules are strict," he said, "and we cannot permit any exceptions. Dollars must be changed into rallods at the other end, so I'm afraid I can't help you."

Allen found himself a chair and sat down slowly.

The travel agent was puzzled at his stricken expression. "If it's as important as all that to get rid of the dollars," he said, "why don't you take another trip and spend them?"

Allen brightened. "Yes. That's the thing to do. How many dollars for two tickets to Centralia?"

"As I told you," the young man said patiently, "foreign currency is handled only by our foreign terminals. Here we deal only in rallods. One thousand rallods for two tickets. When would you like to leave?"

"I'll think about it," Allen said.

Back in the hotel room, Allen and Ann sat staring at each other.

"Thanks to the bellhop, I have eleven rallods," Allen said. "Our hotel bill will be fifteen plus the price of two meals. Twenty-five, at least. And we need a thousand to get back. Got any ideas?"

She shook her head. "It looks as if we'll have a long stay here. And it's not going to be any honeymoon. We'll have to work and earn the money."

"We might as well go up and check out and confess to the manager," Allen said. "Maybe he'll give me some help in getting a job."

"Couldn't we just stay here?"

"Too expensive. Over a hundred rallods a week for the room and that doesn't include meals. And we'll need clothes. I haven't any idea of how much people are able to earn in this crazy world."

Grimly they descended on the room clerk. "Checking out, I see," he said. "Account settled at that window."

A young lady itemized their bill and read off the items. "Room, one day, fifteen rallods. Dinner, by room service, eleven rallods," Allen winced. "Breakfast, three rallods. Total, twenty-nine rallods. Please receipt this bill."

"How was that again?" Allen asked.

Before he quite knew what was happening, his right thumb had been inked, impressed, and wiped clean. Ann contributed her print, and as Allen was struggling for words to explain that he had only eleven rallods, the young lady briskly counted bills out across the counter toward him.

"Twenty, twenty-five, twenty-nine. Thanks very much, sir. I hope you'll stop with us the next time you're in town."

They staggered away from the window, left the hotel, and walk half a block before either of them spoke.

"They paid us," Allen said.

Ann said nothing.

"And the bellhop tipped me."

Ann stopped and pointed at a shop. "Women's apparel. I need a change of underwear."

They entered the shop. Ann made a few modest purchases. The clerk paid her six rallods. They went out.

"Another hotel?" Allen asked.

"Yes. We'll get the most expensive room we can find."

"We might ask for the bridal suite."

"You'd shock them. They might think we were married."

"Isn't there anything more expensive than a hotel suite? Let's find some kind of rental agent and see."

They found a rental agent. He arranged a week's sublease on a luxurious apartment, rent four hundred rallods, paid to them in advance. He also paid them his commission, which was forty rallods. He engaged a maid and a cook for them, and the two servants happily handed their week's wages to Ann when they reported for work.

Allen and Ann went on a reckless shopping tour. They bought luggage, for which they left their thumbprints and were paid a hundred and fifty rallods.

Allen selected a fine new suit and the beaming clerk took his thumbprint and paid him ninety-five rallods. They outfitted themselves completely and returned to their apartment.

"We have our thousand rallods," Allen said. "We can leave any time."

Ann looked about the dazzling living room and gazed sadly at the fountain that bubbled in a far corner. "Yes, I suppose we can."

"We really should be getting back. Doris will have her hands full."

"Yes, I suppose she will."

Allen seized her roughly. "Hang, Doris! We never had a proper honeymoon. Let's have it now. Sue can handle things for a week. She won't like it, but she can do it."

"Let's," Ann said happily. "Who can say when we'll be able to afford anything like this again?"

Allen embraced her fondly. "Paradise!"

"No," Ann said. "Esidarap."

They made it a week to remember. They flitted from nightclub to nightclub. They ran up staggering bills and exchanged their thumbprints for cash when they left. The waiters tipped them lavishly. They attended the theater and received cash along with their tickets. They shopped, after the first sensation of awe wore off, only for compact expensive items that they could carry back with them. They almost become accustomed to starting a meal with dessert and finishing up with an appetizer. They gradually got used to backward-running clocks, a calendar that worked in reverse and riding down to their forty-fifth floor. It was, indeed, Esidarap.

At the end of the week they were still in a mood of unrestrained happiness, but reluctantly ready to return to their normal world and go back to work. And on the fateful seventh day a fist descended rudely upon their door, followed by two heavy-set official-looking men who brushed their frightened maid aside and stood looking them over coolly.

"I.B.F.," one of them said, showing his credentials. "We have been reliably informed that you two are unemployed. Is that correct?"

"Yes, we're unemployed," said Allen.

"We've come to talk to you about your employment compensation."

Ann giggled foolishly and Allen muttered, "All this, and Esidarap too!"

"We are in the process of checking your past record to see if you are paid up to date. But we've established that the compensation is unpaid for the past week and we are here to collect that now. For the two of you, that amounts to seven thousand rallods. Cash or a certified check, please."

Allen choked suddenly on nothing at all and glanced at Ann's white face. "You mean we owe..."

"Every now and then people try to slip away and cheat the government," the I.B.F. agent said. "But they soon find out that it's rather expensive not to work. It you'll take my advice, you'll go back to wherever it is you came from, and go to work, and pay your wages like a good citizen. Right now I want seven thousand rallods."

"My gawd!" Allen groaned. "I wonder what the income tax amounts to!"

The agent was momentarily flustered. "Well, now—that would take some time to check. Better just pay us and let the income tax wait."

Allen got out his wallet and counted. "I have four thousand, five hundred and twenty rallods," he said miserably. "Ann?"

THE BEST OF BIGGLE | 83

She was searching through her purse. "Twenty-one hundred rallods," she said.

"Leaving you three hundred and eighty short," the I.B.F. man said.

"If you'll come with us," Allen told him, "we'll make a couple of purchases and pay you off."

They bought a diamond ring for Ann—her third—and paid the I.B.F. men. Despondently they returned to their apartment, and found the rental agent waiting for them. A quiet, white-haired fatherly sort of man, his face was mournful.

"You two have disappointed me," he said.

"How so?" Allen asked.

"I hoped you would be able to take this place for the summer. But now..." He shook his head. "Why did you do it?"

"Do what?"

"Live so recklessly. I don't know what sort of wages you pay in your normal occupation, but even if it is above average, you've used up your luxury and entertainment allowances for years. You'd have been stopped, of course, if you hadn't done it so fast. But all in one week! The reports are tabulated now and I must ask you to leave."

"How do you know all about it?" Allen demanded.

"My dear young man, why do you suppose your thumbprint is taken with every purchase? All bills go to central accounting and a full statement of purchases is compiled as often as the volume merits. With due estimates, naturally, for such unreceipted items as tips and the like. Surely you knew that."

"Yeah," Allen said, "Surely I knew that."

"So—you must leave. You'll be living at a mere subsistence level for a long time. But—" he shrugged—"when you get your credits back, come and see me again. Perhaps I can arrange something just as nice as this—if you promise to conduct yourselves reasonably." He left mumbling over his shoulder that they were to be out by noon.

"There goes four hundred rallods a week," Ann said.

"Yes, and it's a long way to a thousand," said Allen. "We should have left when we had it."

"I hate to think so," Ann said, "but I guess we should have. It has been fun, though."

"What do we do now?"

The answer came in the form of a performance by the beautifully toned door chimes. It was a detective with a summons. An hour later they were in court. An hour and fifteen minutes later they were tried, convicted and lectured soundly by the judge.

The judge's lecture gave them some insight into what Allen called Backward Economics. They were, the judge informed them, a blight posed to strike at the roots of the entire economy and bring it toppling down. Their offense seemed to be: first, that they had received more for purchases then they were spending in wages; and second, that they were unemployed, and therefore not spending anything in wages.

Allen had a sudden inspiration. "But, Your Honor," he protested, "I couldn't find a job."

His Honor flushed angrily and shattered his gavel with one vicious stroke. "This court will not tolerate such a fiction. You know perfectly well that any citizen who is unable to find employment privately can pay wages to the government."

Allen considered informing His Honor that they were not citizens and thought better of it.

But their sentence did not seem unduly severe. His Honor placed them on probation, banged a fresh gavel and called for the next case.

A burly police officer let them out of the courtroom and into the small anteroom, where the white-robed technicians took charge of them, got them seated at a table, and before they quite knew what was happening had their right thumbs clamped in a small boxlike device.

"The judge said probation," Allen said in indignation. "He didn't say anything about thumb screws."

"Quite a card, aren't you?" the police officer sneered.

Allen felt a sudden stab of pain, nothing more. At the same time Ann winced and looked over at him, puzzled.

"All right," the police officer said. "You can go now." He chuckled. "And don't do it again."

On the steps of the courthouse they stopped to examine their thumbs. Neatly engraved on each was a small P.

"I'll be damned," Allen said. "They've branded us."

They went to the office of their rental agent and that gentleman greeted them with obvious displeasure. "What do you want now?"

"We'll have to live somewhere," Allen said. "We thought perhaps you..."

"I don't handle rentals in your class."

"Couldn't you refer us to someone?"

The man sighed and buzzed his secretary. "These people are on probation," he said. "See if you can find them something."

The secretary departed, giving them contemptuous glances over her shoulder.

"This may sound like an odd question," Allen said, holding up his thumb, "but would you mind explaining this probation business?"

"Try and buy something," the rental agent said. "You will understand it soon enough. You can't make a purchase without receipting it with your right thumbprint. A probation print is not acceptable unless accompanied by a waiver of probation officially certified by the court."

"What do they want to do?" Allen said hotly. "Starve us?"

"Oh, you can buy essentials—the bare essentials. You must register at one store and make all your food purchases there. You can buy clothing, but only such clothing as is necessary for your work, and your employer must furnish a requisition. I don't know the exact amount of your excess, of course, but if you behave yourselves for a few years, the court may take your good behavior into consideration."

"I see," Allen said. "Tell me one thing. Are there any lending institutions around here?"

"I don't understand."

"Banks, loan companies..."

"Oh. You mean borrowing institutions. Certainly—there are plenty of them around. Why do you ask?"

"I'd like to borrow a thousand rallods."

"My dear young man! Were you born yesterday? You don't borrow money from those institutions. You lend them money!"

"Why, yes, of course." Allen said. "Naturally."

The secretary returned and handed Allen a slip of paper. "There's the address," she said. "It isn't much. Just a furnished room. The neighborhood is poor, and it's a walk-down, but I don't think you can do any better than that."

"Thank you," Allen said, "for everything. Does the government confiscate the things we bought?"

"Certainly not," the rental agent said. "The government merely keeps you from buying more until you have retired the excess."

They attempted to transport their belongings by taxi, but the driver took one look at the "P" that registered neatly in the center of Allen's thumbprint and drove off without them. They made four trips by bus, and learned later that they had used up their week's quota. Their new landlady was fat, owlish-looking, and hideously suspicious.

"One of those, eh?" she said, studying Allen's thumbprint. "Well, all right. But I'll have you know this is a decent house, and if the police start nosing around here, out you go." She paid him for a week in advance —six rallods.

They got settled in their cramped room and Allen sat in the lone chair, feeling miserable, while Ann stretched out on the bed and sobbed.

"We'd better get something to eat," Allen said finally.

"I'm not hungry."

"We'll still have to buy some food. If we don't, we won't have any money to pay our wages with, and we can't go to work. And if we don't go to work, we'll have to pay another seven thousand rallods in unemployment compensation at the end of the week. And where will we get the seven thousand rallods?"

She got up wearily. "All right. We'll buy some food, but I won't eat it. And we ought to start looking for jobs."

They registered at a neighborhood grocery store and bought their entire week's allowance of groceries, concentrating on canned good that would not require cooking. They took their groceries, and seventeen rallods, back to their room.

"Now we have twenty-three rallods," Allen said. "That means we can't afford jobs that cost more than eleven and a half rallods."

"You take thirteen," Ann said, "and I'll take ten."

They found an employment agency and went their separate ways for interviews and classification. Allen's interviewer scowled at the blemished thumbprint, scowled at Allen, and shrugged disgustedly.

"Hardly worth the trouble, bothering with one like you," he said. "You need the lowest-paying job you can find. Some kind of sales job might do it. You pay a small guaranteed salary and a commission on what you sell. If you don't sell much, you might get along. It better be something that isn't expensive, because one big sale a week would ruin you. This might do it – cemetery plots. Here's the address. And here—" he handed Allen five rallods—"is the agency fee. I hope we won't see you again."

Ann was already back at the room when Allen returned that evening. She was lying face down on the bed and she did not look up when he came in. He seated himself in the chair and put his feet up on the bed.

"I'm a salesman," he said. "I'm selling cemetery plots. They cost a hundred and fifty rallods each—or, rather, the person that buys one is paid a hundred and fifty rallods. I'm on salary and commission. I pay the boss fifteen rallods a week, and I pay the customer fifteen rallods of that hundred and fifty for every plot I sell. I don't intend to sell any."

She spoke with her face muffled in a pillow. "I'm a filing clerk. It was the best I could do, and it's twenty-five rallods a week. I didn't have the twenty-five, and I have to bring the rest tomorrow or I'm out of a job. All I had was fifteen—ten from the groceries and five from the unemployment agency. I almost got fired anyway, because using the alphabet backwards confuses me."

"Did you try the new clothes angle?"

She sat up. "What's that?"

"I told my boss this was the only suit I had. He thought it looked pretty good –it ought to, since it cost two hundred rallods –but he agreed that a salesman should have more than one suit. He gave me a requisition and I bought a new suit for forty rallods. That's the most expensive one they'd let me have. So it gives us a little margin. You can pay your other ten rallods tomorrow and then…"

"We're getting six rallods a week for this room," Ann said tonelessly. "We're allowed seventeen for groceries. That's twenty-three. And I have to pay twenty-five in wages and you have to pay fifteen. How can we save a thousand rallods, if we go in the hole seventeen every week?"

"You see if your boss will give you a requisition for some clothes and I'll check around. Maybe I can think of some angles.

Maybe they'll let me take a prospect out to dinner now and then. I could pick up a few rallods that way. And maybe something will turn up."

Catastrophe struck the next day, when Allen sold a cemetery plot. "Practically took the thing away from me," he moaned. "I tried insulting him, and knocking the location, and everything else I could think of, but I couldn't get out of it. So there go fifteen rallods."

"I bought twenty-five rallods worth of clothing," Ann said, "so we're still a little ahead. My wages are paid for next week. But you'd better not sell any more."

"I won't," Allen promised. "I'll turn and run first."

They started the second week with their wages honorably paid, and enough surplus to carry them a third week, providing Allen sold no plots. Beyond that lay blank despair.

Allen returned to their room in a fretful mood. He had narrowly avoided making a sale that morning. His evasion tactics were so obvious that the prospective customer complained to his boss. The boss had studied Allen's sales record, which was not impressive, and threatened to discharge him. Allen was tired, discouraged, and nauseated at the thought of another cold meal out of cans. He was homesick for a glimpse of blue sky.

He lurched through the door and halted in amazement.

Ann had a visitor –a bulky, bearded, bald-headed visitor, who learned back in the rickety chair and regarded him quizzically. It was Mr. Gloob, of the Gloob Travel Agency.

Mr. Gloob pointed an accusing finger. "You shouldn't have done it!"

"You're telling me!" said Allen.

Ann leaped up excitedly. "We just got here. I saw him in the street and he almost got away from me. I must have chased him two blocks."

"Three blocks," Mr. Gloob said. "My mother warned me not to pay any attention to strange women, so I tried to ignore her. Unsuccessfully, I might add. But you shouldn't have done it. Do you realize the confusion you've created in our accounting department? Two return trips with no outgoing prints to match with them. The directors have held three emergency meetings and the problem seemed utterly incapable of solution. You'll have to go back you know. You must promise absolute secrecy and leave at once. I won't have it any other way."

"Neither would I," Ann said fervently.

Gloob was studying the room critically. "Why are you living in such a queer place? I've often wondered what people from your world would do in our civilization, but this is not at all what I imagined."

"It isn't what we imagined, either," Allen said, and briefly described their week of reckless living and the depths to which they had fallen.

Gloob raised his arms in horror. "My word! But why did you let them put you on probation and try to live like this? This is terrible! Why didn't you just go back to Centralia?"

"How could we?" Allen demanded. "The I.B.F. men took every bit of our money. We didn't have the thousand rallods for tickets."

Gloob rose slowly to his feet. "My dear friend Allen! Surely you couldn't live in our civilization for over two weeks and have so little understanding of our ways. You do not pay a thousand rallods for tickets. We pay *you* the thousand rallods!"

"But I thought..." Allen began weakly. "I mean, you charged at Centralia, and I paid you, so naturally..."

"I'll start packing," Ann said.

"I'll help you," Allen told her.

Gloob held up his hand. "Just a moment now. Not so fast. This thing is more serious than you realize. You could have gone back at any time before you were put on probation, just by presenting yourself and giving us a receipt. But now you can't give us a receipt. You've used up your allowance of luxuries and it will be a long time before your thumbprints can be honored."

"You mean we're stuck here?"

"That's exactly what I mean. You have no understanding of our economy, of course, or you wouldn't have gotten into trouble. People keep a very careful record of their purchases. If they want some special luxury, like a Boolg tour, they conserve their allowance ahead of time, or they reduce their luxury expenditures drastically after they return. Conduct such as yours is rare. It's considered a serious crime, which is why the punishment is so severe."

There was a long silence while Allen glared at Gloob and Ann looked quietly at the floor.

"All right," Allen said. "Ann, this nonsense has gone far enough. We'll go down to the authorities the first thing in the morning and tell them what happened and ask them to get us away from here."

"Oh, I say!" Gloob exclaimed. "You can't do that. There'd be all kinds of unfavorable publicity for Boolg, Incorporated. We might lose our franchise. We specifically agreed that our operations would be kept secret in your world."

"Tough," Allen said. "If you'll excuse us, Mr. Gloob, we have some packing to do."

"Look, now. Things are developing nicely and we are getting new terminals set up in Europe and South America. You'd spoil everything. At best we'd have to shut down our United States terminals, and that's the most popular place for tours. You have no idea what those tours mean to our people. To pay a hotel bill instead of being paid, to pay for transportation, to pay for food, to work and have the employer pay the – why, it's positively..."

"It's a dirty shame," Allen agreed. "Now if you'll excuse us..."

Gloob sighed. "All right. I'll manage it some way. Go ahead and pack."

Allen reached for a suitcase. "I don't see why you make such a problem out of it. All you have to do is smuggle us away from here. You don't have to pay a thousand rallods to us. What would we do with them?"

"Mmmm—yes," said Gloob. "Perhaps it can be done without any official record made of it. We'll see."

A heavy fist rattled their door and the landlady's rancorous voice called, "Phone call for Mr. Allen!"

Allen started. "I don't know anybody here. Who'd be calling?"

"Why don't you answer it and find out?" said Ann.

Allen plodded up three flights of stairs and apprehensively picked up the telephone. "Hello."

"This is Agent Senoj of the I.B.F. You'll remember our discussion a week or so ago on unemployment taxes."

"For your information," Allen said, "I am now employed."

"I know. At the time you mentioned income tax. We've conducted an investigation and we find that you have received no income taxes for the past five years. The statute of limitations permits no claims of more than five years to be made against the government, but as long as we've definitely established this five-year delinquency, we would like to make a settlement with you."

"Well, that's nice of you," Allen murmured.

"We don't know how this could have happened, but it did happen, and I'd like to have you sign the necessary papers and accept a check in final payment."

"How large a check?"

"With interest and penalties, it comes to twenty-five thousand rallods."

"You don't say. Give me your office address and I'll look you up in the morning."

"What's wrong with this evening?" the agent said.

"I'm busy right now," Allen said. "Meal time you know."

"How about an hour from now?"

"Make it two hours." Allen glanced at his watch and counted on his fingers. "Four o'clock."

"That's a little late, but—all right, expect me at four." Allen hurried back down the stairway. "I.B.F.," he said. "They want to give us twenty-five thousand rallods in back income tax."

"Good heavens!" Gloob breathed. "You aren't serious?"

"Absolutely. He's coming at four."

"We'll have to get you out of here. If the government gives you that much money, it will also have to give you jobs to let you spend it, and that means high executive positions, and you'll never get away. Here, I'll help you pack."

They left in a rush, dashing up the stairs and waiting on the porch while Gloob hurried out into the street to hail a taxi. The landlady charged out of a hallway.

"Just what I expected of scum like you!" she shrieked. "Trying to sneak out on me. Just what I expected. But I been keeping my eyes open, I have. Here –one week's rent for leaving without notice."

She handed Allen six rallods.

They returned to Centralia and the Globe Travel Agency, and the rambling California redwood ten-room ranch house with a rustic lake view, and settled down to a peaceful existence. They never bothered to explain their mysterious absence, and in time their friends tired of asking. And if their friends thought it odd that they named their son Kroywen, none of them mentioned it within their hearing. Not even the boy's godfather, Mr. Gloob.

The business of the Globe Travel Agency expanded at a rate that was absolutely indecent. Allen chartered buses, trains and planes, planned guided tours, and applied all of his ingenuity in the arrangement of colorful itineraries for visitors from another world. Centralia accepted the tourist boom philosophically and credited it to Allen's genius for travel management.

There were no more visitations from strangers requesting accommodations for tongue-twisting places. Mr. Gloob explained that this unfortunate confusion resulted when travelers already on tour attempted to locate the new Centralia terminal and were misled by the similarity in names.

A warm friendship developed between Mr. Gloob and the Allens. Mr. Gloob was frequently a visitor in their home and they had delightful conversations upon all subjects except the world of Mr. Gloob's origin. Only once did Allen tactfully refer to his and Ann's strange pilgrimage.

"I wondered when I was there," he said, "but I never got around to investigating. But the Empire State Building—you call it just the opposite, of course, but I won't try to pronounce that—is a hundred and two stories deep, and yet there's an observation gallery at the bottom."

Gloob, rocking peacefully, smoking his pipe, and watching his godson kick fretfully in a playpen, nodded. "Why, yes, I believe there is."

"Just what do people observe from that observation gallery?"

"They observe more or less the same thing people observe when they look out the windows of buildings."

"But there weren't any windows in buildings!"

Merriment flashed in Gloob's eyes. "Weren't there?" he said.

LESSON IN BIOLOGY

First published in *Fantastic Universe Science Fiction* **November 1957**

I spotted Johnny Kaiser in a little dump of a bar down on South Ashley Street. He was huddled in a rear booth, with a dozen empty beer bottles on his table, and a woebegone, half-drunken expression on his face. He'd sprouted a scraggly mustache since I last saw him. I wondered if it was meant to be a disguise.

You should remember Johnny. If you don't maybe you'd recognize his picture. It was on the front page of every paper in the country. There was that television ceremony, too, when they gave him the ten thousand dollars reward money.

He's the cop that caught the Martians. Remember?

Of course they weren't really Martians. Nobody ever figured out exactly where they came from, but a lot of people called them Martians, and still do. And Johnny caught them.

I squeezed into the booth opposite Johnny, and said, "How's the old Martian chaser?'

He glared at me. "Scram!" he said. But I hadn't seen him since he got the ten grand—in fact, since he'd caught the Martians—so I hung around and watched him put away another bottle of beer.

"With all that reward money, don't tell me you got troubles!" I said finally.

He set his glass down with a bang, and leaned across the table, "My wife left me," he said. "Every place we went, people were saying I didn't really know that dame was a Martian—I just followed her because she was a good-looking dame. Whenever a girl came along, someone would nudge me, and say, 'How about it, Johnny—another Martian?' And then some bum phoned my wife anonymously and said I was being transferred to the women's division so I could keep on looking for Martians. She got sore and left."

"How did you know that dame was a Martian?" I said.

He straightened up, and for a minute I thought he was going to start throwing bottles. But he didn't. He leaned across the table, and said, "Those Martians—they didn't have no sex."

I grinned. "Everyone that saw that dame said she was about the most sexy creature they'd ever seen."

"Sure, sure. She—I mean it—looked sexy. They could look any way they wanted to. Maybe the scientists understand that, now that they got some corpses to study, but they aren't talking. Anyway, I think this Martian saw a picture of a real sexy girl in a magazine, or somewhere, and just went around looking like that."

"And fooled heaven knows how many thousand people until Johnny Kaiser saw her," I said. "And Kaiser took one look, and said, 'There's a Martian!'"

Johnny held up one finger at the waiter. That's his idea of an insult. If I wanted to drink with him, I could buy my own. I held up a finger, and we each got a beer.

"Remember when all this started last April?" Johnny said. "All the papers were screaming about the flying saucer landing. Air Defense picked it up when it came barreling in from the Gulf of Mexico. Before a single jet got into the air over New Orleans, it'd already been lost in northern Wisconsin. And they had the army, and the air force, and the National Guard, and God knows what else looking for it. They didn't find anything, of course, and after while the excitement quieted down, and people forgot about it. Just someone having hallucinations, they said.

"The F B I kept right on checking, because the F B I knows that radar doesn't have hallucinations. In the meantime, those Martians were all over the place, looking like ordinary people, and nobody suspected anything. They'd have gotten away with it, too, except they didn't have no sex and they couldn't understand how it worked with us. They'd have gotten away with it anyway, except that one of the Martians pulled a boner."

I poured the rest of my bottle into the glass and held up two fingers. "I didn't hear about that," I said.

"It was kept quiet. But one of the Martians stayed a couple of weeks in a little rooming house over in Cheboygan, and when it moved out it left a notebook behind. The F B I got ahold of that notebook, and had it studied. The paper was some kind of stuff that the scientists couldn't analyze. The writing was strictly out of this world. And perfectly recorded on those pages were dozens of finger marks, smooth, elongated finger marks. Finger marks without finger prints!

"That tipped the F B I off to the fact that the Martians were going around looking like ordinary human beings. They alerted all police departments in this country and Canada and that was when I heard about the Martians—or aliens, as the F B I called them.

"An F B I man came through and briefed us. 'I think,' he said, 'the thing that will solve this for us is psychology. Even if these aliens look like humans, their psychology is bound to be worlds away from ours. Somewhere along the line, no matter how human they look, they're going to act peculiar. Be on the lookout for that.'

"We were ordered to watch for anyone acting out of character, or getting nosey about commonplace things. I thought that a little newspaper publicity would have turned up the Martians in short order. The Chief said no. Everyone and his brother would be imagining Martians. There would be a general panic, and the real Martians would know we were on to them. I see now that he was right. Even as it was, a lot of mildly eccentric citizens were hauled in for questioning.

"Anyway, I was vaguely on the lookout, never dreaming it would be me that spotted one of them. We got word that Spoofs Hamblin was back in town. I was working plain clothes at the time, and I dropped around to see him. He was staying at the Crown Hotel, which is a little dump of a building that serves as a natural collecting place for the scum that drifts into our fair city. I had a quiet talk with Spoofs. We didn't have anything on him that we could prove, but he wasn't certain about that. I managed to convince him that he and Crown City should go their separate ways, and then I went down and sat in the deserted lobby to see if I could spot any other objectionable characters.

"And in walked the dame. Classy. Long, silky-looking blonde hair. A dress that was practically screaming Fifth Avenue. A figure that was downright sultry, and a face you'd have to call beautiful.

"She walked over to the window and stood looking out for a few minutes, and then she headed for the stairway. No elevators in the Crown.

"I went over and woke up the room clerk. 'Who's the dame?' I said.

"She'd disappeared by then, but he knew who I meant. He whistled.

" 'That one,' I said. 'Who is she?'

" 'Miss Mary Smith. Don't get one like that very often.'

" 'You've never had one like that, and you know it,'" I said.

"I went over to the pay phone, and called headquarters. 'I'm at the Crown Hotel,' I said, 'and I've just spotted a Martian.' I wasn't guessing. I knew."

"You took one look at that sexy dame," I said, "and you knew she didn't have any sex?"

He scowled and I let him tell it his way. "I didn't know, then, about their not having no sex," he said, "I found that out later."

All of a sudden I felt horrified. I stood up. "Kaiser! Just how did you find out she had no sex?"

"Sit down," he said, and I sat.

"They put a team on it," he went on, "and we took turns tailing her. A lab team went over her room while she was out, and found a lot of those smooth finger marks, so we knew we were on the right track. The F B I moved in to supervise, and I got a promotion that was about four years overdue. We could have picked her up, of course, but we wanted her to lead us to the others.

"She never noticed that she was being tailed. Maybe all humans look alike to a Martian. Anyway, she spent some time in the library, and went on a free tour of the local brewery, and went to the movies a couple of times. Every now and then she'd call a cab and have herself driven out to the edge of town, and then she'd call another cab and have herself driven back. I never figured that out, unless she just liked to ride in cabs.

"She nosed around looking things over for a few days, and then one afternoon she checked out of the hotel, and took a cab to the bus station. I was in line behind her when she bought a ticket to Minneapolis. I bought a ticket to Minneapolis. I was in line behind her when she got on the bus. She took a seat by the window, and I sat down beside her. I wasn't taking any chances on her getting away without my knowing it.

"Just before we left I recognized an F B I man talking to the driver, and the driver took a good look at the girl and me and nodded. As we pulled out of the station, I counted four police cars waiting in the street, and as soon as we were out of town I saw a helicopter circling overhead. Once a bunch of jets flew over. Someone a lot higher up than me wasn't taking any chances on her getting away, either.

"We rode west for maybe seventy or eighty miles, and it was just getting dark when she got off the bus out in the middle of nowhere. I waited until the driver was about to pull away, and then I dashed down the aisle and followed her. She was walking away down a side road, and I waited to give her a start. Then a car pulled up with the Chief and an F B I man.

"'We don't just want the girl,' the Chief said. 'We want the whole bunch, and most of all we want their ship. We'll try to stay with you, but we might lose you in the dark. Stay close to the girl, and if you spot the ship, throw this. There'll be plenty of us around to take over.'

"He handed me a grenade. 'What is it?' I said. 'A thermite grenade.' He said. 'It's fixed to make a big flash when it goes off, and it'll keep on burning for quite a while. Long enough. And it won't be easy for them to put out.'

"I started off down the road after the girl. It was really getting dark so I had to close the gap somewhat to keep her in sight. She walked past a couple of farm houses, and took another side road. I could hear the helicopter above me, though it was getting too dark to see. I signaled upward with a penlight I carried, and hoped the pilot would get the idea that we were turning.

"She walked for maybe a mile along the road, with me hugging the side and keeping off into the shadows. She turned off, finally, at a grass-grown driveway. There was a house there, and a barn, and I gathered that they were more or less deserted, though I couldn't see much. I heard the house door open and close. I signaled upwards once more, and then I started out working in towards the house.

"It was an odd night—dark and cloudy, but now and then the moon would break through the clouds and there would be some light. I got close enough to see that the windows on the house were boarded up. I was wondering what I should do next, and the problem was solved for me. Neatly. A heavy masculine voice said, 'You will come inside, please.'

"Something glittered in his hand. It didn't look like a gun, but I had a hunch it would be effective enough. I walked ahead of him very quietly.

"The rooms were bare and dusty, except for the living room, where eight or ten people were talking quietly in groups of two or three. It might have been a cocktail party, minus the drinks, or the aftermath of a PTA meeting—except for the language. Just an average gathering of people, some tall, some short, some thin, some fat. And there was Miss Smith, of course, who would have stood out in any gathering.

"The fellow that nabbed me nudged me out into the middle of the room. He looked like a prosperous business man, with grey hair, pot belly, and a conservative, expensive-looking suit. The others turned and stared, and then Miss Smith recognized me. She'd had plenty of time to look me over during that bus ride. She started to talk, and then the others chimed in, and the words flew pretty fast for a while—odd, hissing words that sounded like nothing I've ever heard before.

"An elderly-looking man stepped forward. 'Why are you here?' he said.

"I had my answer all ready. "I saw this young lady on the bus,' I said. "I don't see a good-looking girl like that every day, so I followed her on the chance I'd get to know her better.'

"They jabbered some more, and then the old man said, 'Why do you want to know her better?'

"I grinned. 'Why do you think?' I said.

"He looked puzzled. He said something, and Miss Smith said something and then they were all talking at once. He silenced them, and started asking questions. What would I do if I got to know her? Would I—kiss her? And so on. I kept my answers as vague as possible, and finally the truth dawned on me. These Martians had no sex, and they just couldn't understand the way it worked with humans.

"They'd been here, then, for five months, studying the human race, and they still hadn't figured out sex. Of course sex was the thing in just about everything they saw—advertising, movies, magazines, books, not to mention the every-day lives of humans, and it had them plenty bothered. They gathered around and gaped, and jabbered like mad every time I answered a question.

"I believe they were rather pleased that a human was sexually attracted to one of them. They seemed to think they were going to get the problem settled right there. In fact, I was afraid they might ask for a demonstration, but they didn't. They just kept asking questions, and I kept making my answers as vague as possible. Another bunch of Martians walked in, and then another. I counted twenty.

"Finally the old man said, 'You would like to know Miss Smith better?'

"'I sure would,' I said.

"'Then you will come with us—with her,' he said.

"I didn't welcome the idea of them taking me home with them to study my sex, but I said, 'Sure. Where is she going?'

"We went outside. There were four cars waiting. 'You will ride with Miss Smith,' the old man said. I heard the helicopter pass overhead, but I had no chance to signal. They'd been so interested in sex, though, that they hadn't searched me. I had my revolver in a shoulder holster, and I had the thermite grenade. I followed Miss Smith into the backseat of a car. The old man and a driver sat in front. The other Martians piled into the other cars, and we were off.

"We drove without lights, and I kept wondering if the helicopter or a police car would spot us. The old man kept looking out the window, but I knew he had his eyes on us. I had to put on an act.

"I took Miss Smith's hand, and the skin was cold and clammy—almost slimy to the touch. It made my flesh crawl.

"She made a quick report to the old man—on what was happening, I suppose. Maybe ten minutes later I gritted my teeth, and made myself put my arm around her. Another progress report. That soft-looking hair brushed against my face, and felt like snakes crawling there.

"I don't know what my next move would have been, if the cars hadn't pulled off to the side and stopped.

'Where are we?' I said.

"'You come with Miss Smith,' the old man said. Very politely, but very firmly.

"We started off across the field. I drew Miss Smith off to one side, thinking that would put me in a better position in case I had to run for it. I walked with my arm around her, and the others watched us with a kind of clinical curiosity.

"We crossed the field, west through a gate, and across another field. I figured my chance for outside help was just about gone. We approached a grove of trees. The moon came out, and I looked around and through the trees and couldn't see a thing of interest. Then we stopped, and there was an odd, crackling sound, and there on the edge of the grove was their ship. I don't know how they had it hidden, but it was plenty effective. And the ship didn't look like a flying saucer—or any of the space ships you see drawings of. It looked more like gigantic bedsprings, with a cabin attached.

"Miss Smith moved forward, and I followed her. When I was close enough, I threw that grenade, and ran like hell. There was a splash of light, and a sudden uproar behind me. I hit the dirt and something snapped over my head. A bush twenty feet away flamed up suddenly, and died down. I crawled behind some rocks, and looked back. The thermite made a steady, blinding glow, and the Martians were hopping around in confusion. I saw one coming out of the cabin with something in his hand. 'Fire extinguisher,' I thought, and I fired twice. He fell, and I emptied my revolver at the rest and started to crawl away. I heard that snapping again, all around me, and some grass on the edge of the grove caught fire.

"Then the jets came in. They really plastered that place, and I was caught in the concussion. When I woke up, I was a hero."

"You were a hero," I said, and I meant it.

"I don't know—I keep wondering if those Martians really meant us any harm. I wonder if they weren't just trying to study us—like a bunch of professors going to Africa to study the natives."

"If so," I said, "they used the wrong approach."

"Yes. And it was kind of stupid of them not to understand sex, even if they don't have none."

"You still didn't tell me how you knew the dame was a Martian."

"I did," he said. "I told you they didn't have no sex and they didn't understand how it works with us."

"So you just took a look at that sexy dame and you..."

"Look," he said. "The Crown Hotel is a dump of a place. The women you see in there are always frowzy, and usually less than honorable. So when you see a really gorgeous doll like that, dressed like a million dollars, you just naturally get curious.

"And you know damn well something's funny when you see her coming out of the wrong rest room!"

ON THE DOUBLE

First published in *Galaxy Magazine*, September 1958

Group Leader Mivar stood rigidly at attention and tried not to think of the maddening itch in the scar tissue at the base of his spine. The unfamiliar, sweltering clothing constricted his limbs and gave him an alarming sensation of impending suffocation. In that moment of extreme discomfort, he allowed himself a treasonable thought.

He did not want to be a hero. He could not recall the precise steps by which he had blundered into this mess, but he wanted out.

General Zort paced back and forth in front of Mivar, flourishing his tail as he pivoted. It was a magnificent tail, long and sturdy, stylishly trimmed. There were rumors that the general dyed his tail, but Mivar couldn't detect any irregularity of color in its glimmering blackness. He allowed his eyes to follow it enviously.

The general noticed this, or perhaps Mivar inadvertently allowed a thought to escape. The general halted.

"Too bad about your tail, Mivar," he said, affectionately caressing his own. "But it had to be done. You understand that. A tail just can't be hidden under those silly clothes."

"I understand, sir," Mivar said.

The itch had become a throbbing torment. He shouldn't have let them do it, he thought. He should have defended his tail with his life. To lose a tail in combat would be bad enough, but to have it sliced off by a doctor, under local anesthesia, was utterly humiliating. There were not enough honors in the Empire to compensate for it. Females would ridicule him. He would lose his coveted position in the Place Guard. How could he parade his men without a tail?

The general was scrutinizing him carefully. "The face is excellent. It is an amazing likeness."

The royal surgeon stepped forward and bowed. "The hearing flaps must be done again," he said. "They are not large enough."

"Not large enough!" Mivar exclaimed.

"Come, now," the general said. "You can have them removed when you return."

Mivar jerked back to attention.

"Vril?" the general said.

The general's chief scientist stepped forward.

"What do you think?"

"It's developing nicely," Vril said. "The preparation will have to be intensive, but I am certain we shall succeed." He whirled on Mivar and spoke in harsh, alien tones. "Who are you?"

Mivar's tongue struggled awkwardly to form the strange words. "I am Major Jeffery Holder, Commander of the First Venus Expedition."

Vril moved to the side of the room and touched a button. Sounds boomed at them. Alien sounds. The voice of an Earthman. "I am Major Jeffery Holder, Commander of the First Venus Expedition."

"Not bad," the general said.

"Certainly it is not bad, "Vril said. "It is also not good, and it must be perfect. But we shall work at it. It will be done."

"And you are certain of success?"

Vril bowed. "As positive as one can be amidst life's many complicated uncertainties."

"Carry on," the general said. He walked majestically away, flourishing his tail. His entourage filed out after him, also with tails waving. As soon as their backs were turned, Mivar's hand leaped to the base of his spine and scratched energetically.

"Now then—" Vril began.

Mivar sat down wearily. Standing was a difficult process, without the aid of a tail. "More?" he said.

"More. Who can tell what situations you must face, what emergencies? Reciting a few statements will not be enough. You must speak the language, and speak it perfectly. You must study this Major Jeffery Holder—study him in his cell, and study the films we have taken. You must talk like him, and walk like him, and act like him. You must even think like him. They did a very good job on your face, and your form is similar to his. But appearance is only the first step. The gods have generously presented us with this opportunity and we dare not blunder. Now then, listen, and repeat the words. Imitate the voice."

He touched the button and the alien voice filled the room. "I am Major Jeffery Holder, Commander of the First Venus Expedition."

And so it went. For half a light-cycle, Mivar slaved under the sharp eyes of Vril. Hidden, he observed Vril's interviews with the captured Earthman. He watched films. He learned to mimic the Earthman's walk, and his gestures and even his facial expressions. The Earthman's recorded conversation was played to him as he slept. And in time, even Vril had to admit that he was becoming proficient.

Somewhere nearby, another officer was studying the other Earthman, Lieutenant Roger Anderson—studying him under the sharp tutelage of Vril's assistants, and making, Vril informed Mivar, excellent progress.

"The first surgery didn't turn out as well as yours," Vril said. "But they have corrected now. It's too bad that stupid patrol had to kill the other three. The odds would be more in our favor if we could send back a full crew of five."

"Why not?" Mivar asked. "We know what they looked like."

"But we don't know what they talked like, or how they acted. There's no point in training an officer and sending him along if he's going to give the entire project away the first time he opens his mouth. No, we'll send back the two of you, and you can regretfully explain that the others were killed in an accident, which is true. Better make it wild animals. They expected wild animals. Now then." He switched to the alien language. "Tell me, Major, what did you find on this planet Venus?"

Mivar delivered a brief lecture, based entirely upon carefully planned misinformation.

General Zort held a meeting at his headquarters to review progress, and as Mivar stood waiting, an Earthman entered the room and approached him. He halted in front of Mivar, snapped to attention, and delivered an Earth salute with his hand.

"Lieutenant Anderson reporting, sir," he said.

"At ease, Lieutenant," Mivar said.

The onlookers applauded, and the lieutenant flashed a thought at Mivar. "Group Leader Hezzit."

"Group Leader Mivar," Mivar flashed back, "Wonder why they kept us apart all this time."

"They didn't want us to get the Earthmen confused."

"But now, "Vril said, "you know your subjects well. Next you must learn how they behave with each other. We are placing them in the same cell, for observation purposes."

General Zort interrupted, "It is time we did some serious planning."

"There are many obstacles,' Vril said, "but in my opinion, it needs only proper planning."

"I am in complete agreement," the general said. "What you have accomplished is astonishing. Do we show Mivar and Hezzit to the Earthmen? I would like to see their reactions."

"Definitely not," Vril said. "We must not let them suspect our plans. Without being aware of it, they are giving us valuable information, and if they become suspicious, they will certainly create difficulties."

"You are entirely correct, as usual," the general said hastily. "Let us discuss these obstacles."

"First," Vril said, "they must learn to operate the ship."

"Obviously."

"This can be done. They will return it to the planet Earth, and a short time before they reach their destination, they will communicate with Earth. They will say their communication device had broken down and they had just succeeded in repairing it. They will place the ship in an orbit near the space station which the Earthmen have circling their planet. This is according to plan, because the Earthmen feared there would not be sufficient fuel remaining for a landing on Earth. Our own calculations confirm this.

"No doubt they will receive a hero's welcome when they arrive on Earth. We confidently expect that they will receive every honor and consideration. So—when they complain of extreme fatigue after their long and trying expedition, it is to be expected that they will be placed in seclusion for the rest which their heroic efforts have earned. We hope this will be done with a minimum of contacts with Earthmen. The fewer the contacts, the less likely it is that their real identities will be discovered.

"At the first opportunity after they are placed in seclusion, they will escape. Disappear."

"Won't that arouse suspicion?" the general asked.

"It will arouse concern, but not suspicion. The Earthmen will believe that the hardship of the expedition has unbalanced them mentally. There will be an intensive search, of course, but it will not be a search for alien spies. It will be a search for two mentally ill Earthmen.

"As soon as Mivar and Hezzit have escaped, they will alter their appearances according to a plan which they will practice. We have studied the captured Earthmen and all reproductions of Earthmen which were found in the ship, and we have devised composite identities which will serve as a satisfactory disguise. There are difficulties that must be worked out, but it can be done. They will disappear. If they have been separated, they can easily arrange to meet, because telepathic communication is known to the Earthmen only as a theory. They will meet, and then they will be able to collect the information we must have."

"Wouldn't it be less risky to have them land on the planet in secret?" asked General Zort.

"The Earthmen have detection devices and an attempt at a secret landing would be highly suspicious," Vril replied. "It might alarm the Earthmen. That is one thing we must avoid."

"Very well," the general said. "And how do they bring the information back to us?"

"A very critical question. We are developing a more compact fuel for the ship. We can arrange secret compartments for it. They will be able to return once they get back to the ship. This will be difficult, whether the ship is left in orbit or whether the Earthmen refuel it and return it to Earth. But Mivar and Hezzit are resourceful and ingenious as we well know. They will find a way. Their return does not worry me. The most critical stage of the operation will occur when they land on Earth. I would like to show you some dream-strips. This one is Major Holder's."

Vril signaled and the screen at the far end of the room flashed to life.

The spaceship had landed. It stood surrounded by a throng of wildly cheering Earthmen. Major Holder appeared in the airlock and clasped his hands above his head.

As he started down the ramp, a figure broke loose from the crowd, dashed up the ramp and hurled itself into his arms.

The scene shifted abruptly. An interior scene. A large sleeping cushion in the background, mounted ridiculously above the floor.

The strange figure clung to the major, who stooped, lifted it and turned.

Vril raised his hand and the screen went blank.

"What follows is disgusting," Vril said.

"What is it?" the general wanted to know.

"An Earth female. That one is Major Holder's mate."

"Ah!"

"You see the problem. The Earthmen have a single mate and they spend their lives in close association. It is likely that their mates know them more familiarly than any of their other associates. The mates will certainly be present to greet them when they return. In my opinion, this is the most dangerous obstacle they will face. If they pass it successfully, our plan must succeed. Here is a dream-strip of Lieutenant Anderson."

In the company of a group of obviously important personages, the lieutenant made his way through a crowd. Guards pushed the cheering spectators aside to make way for them. Suddenly the lieutenant turned, battled his way into the crowd, and clasped a female in his arms.

Vril stopped the picture with a wave of his hand. "There are exaggerations and inaccuracies in a dream-strip, of course, but by comparing enough strips we can obtain an excellent idea of how to surmount this obstacle. The females alter their appearances in subtle ways, but Mivar and Hezzit must be able to recognize these mates of Major Holder and Lieutenant Anderson under any circumstances. If the mates do not come to them on the landing, they must seek them out. The greeting can be brief and undemonstrative, but there must be a greeting, and the mates must be convinced."

"What about afterward?" Mivar said, squirming nervously on his cushion. The sight of the room with the sleeping cushion had incited an apprehensive itching in his scar tissue.

"You are tired. You need rest. Even the presence of your mate would be disturbing to you. You might even be ill. There shouldn't be any problem about afterward. But you must greet the mates properly, according to Earth custom. Not to do so would be fatal."

Hezzit said uneasily, "We must—"

"It is called a kiss," Vril said. "The mouths meet. The Earthmen have no tails, as you well know. They use the kiss as a substitute. Come—certainly you will not allow a mere Earth female to stand in the way of our glorious conquest."

"Does the Earthman say anything to his mate?" Mivar asked.

"As you might expect from a species that does not have thought contact, the Earthman says much. You will be well rehearsed on that point. I have compiled all of the dream-strips in which the mates appear. And there are many of them. We will add others as we record them. It is unfortunate that the Earthmen lost all of their personal possessions in the river crossing when they were attempting to escape our patrol. I understand that they had life photos of their mates, and there is always a danger that the appearance of these Earth females may be exaggerated or modified in the dream-strips.

"But we can make the dream-strips serve our purpose. You will watch now, Mivar, and remember that you must be able to recognize Major Holder's mate, and you must know how to manage the greeting."

They ran the dream-strips, Major Holder's and Lieutenant Anderson's.

Mivar had the major's mate so thoroughly impressed into his conscious and subconscious mind that even he dreamed of her. The major called her Sally. He dreamed of her in a variety of odd settings, both public and private. The dream-strips showed them going through the pointless motions which were called dancing, striking a ball with a stick in some absurd test of skill, swimming, dressing or undressing, usually with each other's assistance.

Hezzit was suffering the same familiarity with Lieutenant Anderson's mate, who was called Kathy.

The ultimate indignity occurred when Vril made them practice the Earthman greeting, the kiss. He made them practice it on each other.

They learned to fly the Earthmen's ship, suffering near-disaster on the takeoff, but successfully placed it in an orbit around their planet. They gazed in awe at their cloud-shrouded home and apprehensively at the distant light in the sky that was Earth. For the first time, they saw the stars. Vril, who accompanied them, made observations and films. Hezzit, a mathematical genius, amused himself by laying out courses for Earth and sarcastically commenting on the inefficiency of the Earthmen's computer.

"Our people have lived in blindness," Vril said. "The ship operates on a simple principle. We could have built one centuries ago, if we had known what lay beyond our sky. We speculated but we did nothing because there seemed to be no purpose. And now—look! Worlds to conquer! Thousands of worlds!"

They were badly shaken up on landing, but suffered no serious damage. They continued to practice, using the fuel that Vril developed.

They traveled long distances in toward the sun, and turned back to explore space on the Earthward side. They used the ship to put a space station in orbit about the clouds of their own planet. They saw the completion of the first of the giant warships Vril had planned, and they tested it, and started the training of the crew that would operate it. They could reasonably call themselves experts. They were ready.

There was an audience with the emperor. His Majesty descended from his throne and presented both group leaders with the Order of the Tail, and as the sparkling insignia was pinned to his Earth clothing, Mivar felt compensated, at least to a degree, for his own lost tail.

More honors—greater honors—would be theirs after they successfully completed their mission, His Majesty informed them. There would be an entire world to divide and honor enough for all.

"When you return," Vril told them, "The invasion fleet will be ready. Our success depends upon yours."

They left for Earth.

A single Earth week from the end of their journey, Mivar broke radio silence. "Morning Star calling Earth," he announced.

There was a blank, nerve-wracking silence, and then the response exploded at him. "Good God, man! We'd given you up. What happened?"

"Transmitter broke down," Mivar said. "We just got it fixed."

"How are you?"

Mivar said laconically, "Three men lost. Holder and Anderson returning. Expect to orbit in seven days."

"How are you holding up?"

"It's been a rough trip, with just the two of us. We're pretty tired. Reserve a couple of rooms for us at the bottom of a coal mine."

"Will do. This is great, just great. Tough about the others, of course, but—what sort of place is Venus?"

"Damp," Mivar said, and signed off.

From the pilot's seat, Hezzit asked, "Everything all right?"

"Seems to be," said Mivar.

"This will be a great triumph for Vril. And he deserves it."

"He certainly gave us a thorough preparation," Mivar said. He remembered one interview with Major Holder, when Vril had asked, "How do you feel after a trip through space?" and the major had replied, "You feel like reserving a room at the bottom of a coal mine." Mivar had memorized and absorbed the major's habits of speech until they were his own. He had memorized the major's own responses to hundreds of situations. Had it not been for the necessity of greeting the major's mate, he would have looked forward eagerly to his visit to the planet Earth.

Hezzit was undergoing similar apprehensions. "This distinctive odor the Earthmen have," he said. "Do you remember it?"

"How could I forget it?"

"Will the Earth females have the same odor?"

"I don't know. I suppose they might. We can try to make it a short greeting."

"I wasn't thinking about that. I can always – what's the Earth expression?"

"Hold your nose."

"Right. I can always hold my nose—mentally, of course. But I was wondering if we have an odor that would be distinctive to the Earthmen."

Mivar caught his breath. "I hadn't thought about that. Vril didn't think of it."

"It's a possibility. One never knows how one might smell to another species. And then—supposing they notice the lack of an Earthman odor?"

"There should be other things to keep their attention away from odors when we land."

"There'd better be."

One hour later, Earth time, General Rysdale, the commander of the Venus Project, called them. Mivar delivered his first report of a nonexistent Venus, and the general absorbed it intently.

"The place sounds like a roaring hell," he announced.

"It certainly is that, sir," Mivar said.

"And you found nothing but those dismal swamps from pole to pole?"

"There are a few low hills in the south-temperate zone, and what might be the remains of a mountain range around the north pole. Nothing much at either place but some rocks sticking up. And the place is hotter than the proverbial underworld."

"Then I guess we won't be sending colonists to Venus."

"I should hope not, sir. If you do, don't ask me to volunteer."

"What did you do for oxygen? You didn't have enough for all the time. It's more than two years since you left."

"There's plenty of oxygen there, sir. It comes mixed with some gases that made the guinea pig drop dead after one whiff. We didn't try it ourselves, but we extracted the oxygen."

"You're sounding good, Holder. How do you feel?"

"Tired," Mivar said. "Very tired. I won't feel like much of anything until I get some rest."

"We'll see that you get it—all you want. How's your health?"

"All right, as far as we know. We're just tired."

The general signed off. The following day, Mivar was asked to dictate an official report on his experiences. He was prepared. He already had it memorized.

After that, they reported their position twice daily, and shrugged off Earth's solicitous interest in their welfare. They orbited on schedule and a small space tug towed them to the space station. They moved down a connecting tube to the station and their first contact with Earthmen.

A colonel met them. Mivar came to attention, saluted snappily and began, "Colonel—"

"Nuts!" the colonel said, clapping him heartily on the back. "You never called me colonel before. Jim is good enough now. Besides, you're a colonel yourself now. Mean to say they didn't tell you?"

Mivar accepted the hand the colonel thrust at him and said, "No. They didn't tell us."

"Maybe the general's keeping it for a surprise. Be sure and let it surprise you, or he might skin me."

He stepped back and scrutinized Mivar. "You don't look bad, fellow, considering what you've been through. I thought you'd be a stretcher case. You look just the same, except you've lost some weight."

"I feel different," Mivar admitted.

"Well, no wonder! You'll get over that. All you need is some rest and some good cooking. But you've accomplished something, fellows. We've been wondering for centuries just what was behind those Venus clouds. Now we know. Nothing but swamp, eh?"

"Not much more than swamp."

"And those big lizards—holy terrors, eh?"

"I suppose you'd call them holy terrors. I don't know that they were lizards. They just looked that way. Jones was our biologist, you know, and we never had a chance to discuss them with him."

"Tough. Poisonous, you say?"

"One swipe of the claws and that was it."

"Tough. I suppose we shouldn't call them lizards. It's natural to try to compare extraterrestrial life with Earth life, but it's probably wrong. What did you call them?"

"Nothing for publication," Mivar said.

The colonel slapped his back again and said, "Well, the rocket is ready to go. How are you, Anderson? Didn't mean to neglect you. It's Captain Anderson, now, you know. I guess we'd better not keep the general waiting—especially since he has a mob of VIPs waiting with him."

They took seats in the rocket ship and strapped themselves down. Hezzit flashed a thought at Mivar. "They don't seem suspicious."

"No reason why they should," Mivar flashed back.

They had passed the first obstacle.

Mivar had time for careful reflection as they dropped Earthward. He remembered the colonel from one of Major Holder's dream-strips, but the major had not given his name. In spite of this, no embarrassment had resulted. The Earthmen had accepted him naturally.

It came to him as a momentous revelation that what they were doing was such a fabulous thing, such an inconceivable thing, that the Earthmen could not possibly suspect. The Earthmen had no reason to believe there was intelligent life on Venus. Even if there were, the Earthmen had no reason to believe it resembled themselves in any way. And if it did—who among them would expect inhabitants of Venus to return in the Morning Star, looking, talking, acting like members of the ill-fated crew, even knowing their inner-most thoughts?

If Mivar were to confess his deception now, they would think him mentally unbalanced. A medical examination would prove otherwise, of course, but Mivar and Hezzit would disappear before they became the subjects of examinations.

He flashed a thought at Hezzit. "It's going to be all right. They can't possibly suspect anything."

Hezzit flashed back nervously, "I think we should have spent more time practicing that kiss."

"You didn't have to remind me," Mivar grumbled.

There were crowds at the landing field. It was much like the tumultuous welcome the returning Earthmen had been accorded in the dream-strips. Mivar, however, had the impression that the onlookers were curious rather than joyful. He walked down the landing ramp, waited for Hezzit, and the two of them moved off side by side.

"How do you feel?" Mivar flashed.

"Like I'll be glad when it's over."

The official welcoming party stood some distance away. The crowd was held back by a rope—Mivar had seen the same arrangement in several dream-strips. There were the photographers, the newsmen and after looking at so many dream-strips, the whole seemed so familiar to Mivar that he had the impression of having been there before.

When they approached the official party, he saw that there were several females among it. He searched their faces anxiously for one, and only one, and failed to find it. As he slowed his steps, one of the females broke away and raced toward them. She threw herself into Hezzit's arms, and Mivar saw with a thrill of satisfaction that Hezzit was handling himself with masterful correctness.

"Everything all right?" Mivar flashed.

Hezzit flashed back, "The thing reeks."

Mivar turned again to the little group that stood waiting. The familiar face, the hauntingly familiar face, was not there. He hesitated with a growing feeling of panic, running his eyes over the crowd that stood watching, quietly.

Suddenly he saw it. There could be no doubt. The female stood in the front line, hands on the rope. It was Holder's mate.

He hurried toward it.

The face was smiling and weeping as he reached it. He stood with the rope between them and took the female into his arms. Its arms tightened around his neck. Its words came to him clearly above the noise of the crowd.

"Jeff! Oh, Jeff. But—you shouldn't have—"

The face brushed his. The lips moved towards his. He knew then that everything was all right. The deception was complete. No one would ever know.

The next moment, pain exploded in his brain.

General Rysdale said, "One dead. What about the other?"

"He just wouldn't be taken alive, sir. Whatever they are, they're some fighters. He took on an entire squad and flattened every one of them. Then he took their guns and started shooting. I didn't think the casualties were worth it, and there was always the chance he'd turn a gun on himself the last minute."

"You're probably right. I doubt that we could have made him talk, even it we'd taken him. If it had to be, it had to be."

"Did you get the report on Holder—I mean the one that looked like Holder?"

"I got it. Extraterrestrial life, highly intelligent and damned cunning. The thing could have fooled Holder's own mother. Colonel Meyers has known Holder all his life and he didn't suspect a thing. Those two were equipped to do a more thorough spying job on this planet than could be imagined. How they were going to get the information back to Venus, I don't know. We'll have to take a careful look at the Morning Star."

"That's being worked on now, sir."

"As for their procedure—I've been wondering about that insistence on a secluded rest. It didn't sound unusual at the time, but now I'm beginning to wonder. They had something planned. They were going to collect information and get it back to Venus. What next? An invasion?"

"I suppose it's possible."

"You're darn right it's possible. They have an incredibly high technology. The miniature photographic equipment this phony Holder was carrying is beyond anything we can make. People with that ability can copy a spaceship and we know darned well they can fly one. They got the Morning Star back here, and they put it in the station's orbit about as slickly as the boys up there had ever seen it done. Well, we're forewarned now. We'll have a few surprises ready for any invaders."

"Since they won't be getting the information, they might not invade."

"That's possible, but we won't count on it. We might even plan a little invading ourselves. We'll throw out that tripe they fed us about Venus, too. Since it has a high civilization, it might even be a nice place to live. Did you talk to the girl?"

"Yes, sir. She says she never knew Holder."

"That was a rather warm greeting for a man she never knew. Check it out. Holder had a reputation as a ladies' man, and I think you'll find she was number one on his list at the time he left Earth."

"I'll check it all the way through, sir."

"It was a good plan they had. We shouldn't underestimate them. It scares me to think how close they came to bringing it off. But—" he grinned and tilted back in his chair—"we had two good breaks. I don't pretend to understand how they happened, but here they are. The first was that Holder had a jealous wife. The second was that this double of Holder's greeted another woman so warmly right under Mrs. Holder's nose. It horrified me at the time, but when I think back on it, it was nothing short of marvelous the way Mrs. Holder grabbed the guard's gun and shot the Venusian dead."

THEY LIVE FOREVER

First published in *Satellite Science Fiction*, March 1959

Before he stepped out of his hut into the clear morning air, Mathews repeated his calculations of the night before. The result was the same. In Earth-time, this was the Day. And if it were not, if an error had crept into his records down through the years, this particular day was close enough. It would do.

He stood looking at the village below him, at the laboriously-cultivated fields on the lower slope, and the peacefully grazing zawye, some of which were still being milked. From the village street the little chief saw him, and raised both hands. Mathews returned the greeting, and took the down path.

The chief approached him humbly. "Is your Day of Days satisfactory?"

Mathews looked down at the breath-taking panorama this strange planet served him each morning with breakfast. The haze of the ground mist was shot through with riotous colors that drifted and spread and changed before his unbelieving eyes. Without warning the jungle would suddenly flip into the sky and hang above itself in a dazzling, inverted mirage. In the distance the broad surface of a mighty river mirrored the pink-tinted clouds of early morning. The sight awed and stirred Mathews as it had on thousands of other mornings, and as it would each morning as long as his eyes served him.

"The day is satisfactory," he said to the chief.

The chief gave a little grunt of satisfaction, and shouted a command.

From nearby huts came warriors, eight, ten, a dozen. They carried an odd miscellany of weapons, and Mathews was responsible for many of them—spears, blowpipes, a boomerang, bows and arrows, and odd items that Mathews had invented. They were resourceful people, these Rualis—quick, intelligent and brave. They reacted with rare enthusiasm to a new idea.

Women came forth to approach Mathews with shy respect. They bowed before him with their gifts. He accepted a skin of sweet wine, bread cakes, and pieces of dried meat. A whispered request and a small boy scurried into a hut and returned with a hoe.

"The Day waits," Mathews said. He took the downward trail, and the Rualis marched behind him, singing lustily.

They moved quickly down the cool, sunny mountain slope, and the torrid heat of the jungle rolled up in waves to meet them. The natives moved ahead of him when they reached the jungle, to protect him from the nameless terrors that lurked there. Mathews had never seen these terrors, and frankly doubted their existence, but he never protested. His ability to yield graciously on matters that were really unimportant was one reason for his success with these people.

The Tree was their objective. It had been a forest giant when Mathews first saw it—fifty-eight years before, by his calculations. The Tree held some mysterious significance for the natives which he had never fathomed. They conducted ceremonies there, and their dancing kept a broad, circular track cleared. But they never invited his presence, and he never attempted to intrude.

The Rualis seated themselves in a circle about the Tree. They had removed their clothing, and perspiration glistened on their suntanned bodies. Insects swarmed around them. Mathews waved his hand in a friendly salute, and turned off the jungle trail. The path he followed was faint, overgrown, almost obliterated. The Rualis never used it, and it had been ten days since his last visit.

He moved a dozen yards into the jungle, slashing at the undergrowth with his hoe, and reached a small clearing. He seated himself on the ground, and drank deeply from the wine skin. Insects droned incessantly overhead, colossal insects, but they did not bother him. That was one of many mysteries of this strange planet. The insects plagued the Rualis, but ignored the Earthman.

Back at the Tree, the Rualis continued their singing. The song tossed swingingly on the breeze, backed up by intricate thumping on a dried liayu fruit. Mathews suspected that they were a highly musical people, though he knew too little about music himself to share their extreme pleasure in it.

He pushed the wine skin aside, and chewed solemnly on a piece of meat, feeling a deep, relaxing peace within himself. It was his day—his birthday, by Earth-time, as well as he had been able to keep it. It was also, by a coincidence he had often pondered down through the years, the anniversary of the tragedy that had placed him on this planet.

The ship had crashed on his sixteenth birthday. It rested somewhere in front of him, hidden by the impenetrable curtain of green. Long years before, the roaring jungle had swallowed it up in its clinging, rusting embrace. It had been years—decades, even—since Mathews had last hacked his way through to visit it. Now he was content to leave it undisturbed. There was nothing entombed there except memories, and the clearing had memories enough to satisfy him.

On the other side of the clearing were the graves—six of them, side by side. At one end Mathews had buried his grandfather. At the other end rested the mortal remains of old Wurr, the immortal man who was not immune to accidents. Between them lay the four-man crew of the Fountain of Youth.

"Seven is a lucky number," his grandfather had said. "Come along, and bring us luck." So Mathews had come, and brought luck only for himself. Of the seven, he alone had survived the crash.

At the time the Fountain of Youth set forth bravely for the far reaches of the galaxy, he'd had little understanding of his grandfather's quest. The adventure, the excitement was enough. He hadn't particularly cared whether they reached their objective or not.

Now he was an old man, and he understood—too well. It was not an idle whim that led his grandfather to name the new star ship Fountain of Youth. Grandfather Mathews quite literally sought the source of eternal life, but his objective was a planet of youth, rather than a fountain. He sought the home planet of old Wurr.

Wurr, the kindly old immortal! Mathews' memory could still search back over the years and bring him vividly to life. Bushy hair, black, twinkling eyes, low, husky voice, he never seemed anything but ordinary.

And the known facts about him were nothing less that staggering.

Wurr had survived a precipitous arrival on Earth when the space ship on which he was a passenger plunged onto the Pacific Ocean. Wurr was found bobbing on the surface in a space suit, the only survivor. He was a mature man then, and from that day until he left Earth on the Fountain of Youth, three hundred and seventy-two years had elapsed. That much was documented history.

He lived forever.

Ordinary man and immortal man, man of simple, unaffected habits, man of mystery. He was a sly and candid observer of the human scene. Historians sought him out—an eye-witness of more than three centuries of Earth's history. He submitted willingly to examinations, but he balked at answering questions. He was no different, he said, from anyone else—where he came from.

Grandfather Mathews became acquainted with him, and reached a conclusion on a subject that had been giving rise to much speculation ever since Wurr had completed his first hundred years on Earth. Wurr's home was a planet of immortality, a planet of perpetual youth.

Supposing an alien, a native of Earth, were to visit that Planet. Would he receive the gift of immortality? Grandfather Mathews conferred with Wurr. The immortal man was reluctant. He liked Earth. Eventually Grandfather Mathews convinced him, and the Fountain of Youth expedition was born. Earth had lately developed star travel, and Wurr knew with the exactitude of a skilled navigator the stellar location of his home planet in the Constellation Scorpio. Grandfather Mathews was confident.

Mathews understood, now, that the old man had not taken him along as a whim. He had frankly sought immortal life for himself, but he was a practical old fellow. He admitted the possibility that he might already be too old, too near to death, to be redeemed by the powers of that miraculous planet. But his grandson, only a boy in his teens—surely the planet could work the miracle for him! That was the legacy the old man had sought for Mathews. Not wealth, not prestige, but immortality. Mathews gazed at the six graves with a searing pang of regret. Perhaps the bones had already dissolved in the moist jungle soil, but he carefully tended the graves as a lasting monument to his own loss, to a loss that seemed more tragic with each passing year as his life drew to a close, to the loss of life itself. But for the stupid accident, he might have achieved that which men of Earth had dreamed of for as long as there had been dreams.

And the life was good. Even on this savage planet it was good. He had been too young when he arrived to feel deeply the loss of the civilized splendors of Earth. His very youth had given him much in common with the child-like Rualis. He had enjoyed love and laughter, the hunt, the occasional, half-coming tribal war. He had helped the Rualis to become strong, and they gave him lasting honor.

Life was good, and it was beating its measured way to the inevitable end, to the damp soil of the jungle. And it might have been otherwise.

Mathews got wearily to his feed, and went to work with the clumsy, stone-bladed hoe. He cleared the green shoots from around the head-stones he had carved with such care so many years ago. The mounds had to be reshaped after every rainy season. The jungle was perennially encroaching upon the clearing. The open ground had been much larger in his younger days, but as he grew older he allowed the jungle to creep back. Now it seemed a struggle to hold the space remaining.

There were times when he thought he should remove the graves to a high, dry place on the mountain side. But this place seemed to belong to them, and they to it—here, where their quest had ended, hundreds of light-years from Wurr's planet of immortality, wherever it might be.

WHO STEALS MY MIND...

First published in *Fantastic*, October 1958

His name was Steve Rennon, his official title was detective-sergeant, and he was an alert-looking young man with reddish hair, a boyish, freckled face, and a slender body that was actually about as frail as that of an adult tiger. His generous expanse of mouth was arranged in a warm, infectious grin. Total strangers who passed him on the street found themselves compelled through some mysterious psychological chemistry to grin back at him, though when he had passed they frequently stopped to stare after him.

If there was anything wrong with the world that sunny spring afternoon, Steven Rennon was not aware of it. He paused at the intersection of Main and High Streets to wait for the light to change, grinning happily at the gay throng of shoppers that gathered around him there at the corner, and running an appreciative eye over the late-model cars that roared past.

Half a block away a bus was building up speed to beat the light. It came thundering towards him, and suddenly Rennon's grin dissolved. He stared at the looming menace of the bus, his lips pressed tightly together, his face pale beneath its galaxy of freckles. A thought leaped into his consciousness and rested there, gnawing and prodding.

"What's the use? What have I got to live for? They're all stupid, greedy fools. Get it over with. This bus—one long step, and then no more worries. Watch it, now. Watch it! Have to time it just right, or the fool driver might have time to stop. Watch it... get ready... *now!*"

* * * *

He jerked himself away, and staggered backwards into the crowd. The light changed, the waiting pedestrians crowded out into the street, and Rennon continued his retreat as far as the polished facade of the First National Bank Building, where he placed a trembling hand against the smooth stone surface to support himself. He rested there, breathing deeply, and shaking his head unbelievingly.

"What a stupid thing to be thinking!" he told himself. "Why, I never..."

But he had thought it. That much he couldn't deny. He had thought it right up to the now, and suddenly the thought had disintegrated into a rancorous, sinister, echoing laugh. He had thought the thought, but he hadn't laughed the laugh. He puzzled it through for perhaps two minutes before he reached a conclusion.

He had thought the thought, and the thought wasn't his.

He said to himself, "Next stop, the state mental hospital. Check your strait jackets, please."

He shook his head again, and stepped away from the building. No sooner had he pointed his mental processes at another try at the intersection, then he found himself face to face with an exceedingly angry young lady. Her face went white, and then red, before his started eyes. It was a highly attractive face, but Rennon did not have time for the briefest of mental whistles.

Because, suddenly, inexplicably, unjustly, and without any warning whatsoever, she slapped him.

It was a good slap, delivered with a robust, circular swing and a slight pivot that enabled her to get her shoulder behind it. Rennon could not remember ever getting slapped more efficiently, even when he deserved it. Inwardly he was all for turning her over his knee and paddling her, but good. Outwardly he grinned benignly at her.

His grin had the happy faculty of broadening when he became angry, and the grin he gave the girl was one of colossal proportions. He said quietly, "Have we met somewhere before?"

The grin had its effect. The girl exclaimed, "Oh!" And then as her face paled, she gasped, "Then it wasn't you!"

"If whatever it was deserved a slap, then it wasn't me," Rennon said.

He looked at the girl approvingly. She stared at him, her lips parted slightly, blank dismay in her face.

"Maybe I can help," he said, showing her his credentials. "What is it that's bothering you?"

"A policeman!" she wailed.

"But a very nice policeman. Now—what's the trouble?"

"Someone said something to me. Something nasty. Then he laughed. I thought it was you."

"He laughed?" Rennon said thoughtfully. He was remembering that explosive command, *"now!"* and the sinister laugh that followed. "Are you sure you *heard* him say it?"

"I thought –what do you mean?"

"I'm not sure what I do mean," Rennon said. "Except that I just had a similar experience. Maybe..."

His words were lost in the urgent shriek of brakes and a piercing scream. Rennon whirled and bounded towards the street. A white-faced motorist leaped from his car. Rennon met him over the crumpled body of a woman.

The motorist lifted his hands helplessly. "She jumped right in front of me!"

Rennon bent over the woman, and when he looked up the girl was standing beside him. "I'm a nurse," she said. "Could I..."

"Sure," Rennon said. "Take over. But I don't think she needs a nurse."

* * * *

He strode angrily at the gathering crowd, forcing it back. A uniformed patrolman sprinted up, breathing heavily. A patrol car squealed to a stop. Rennon searched through the crowd looking for witnesses, and scribbled names and addresses. When he looked again at the victim, the girl was kneeling beside her on the pavement. She had the woman's arms neatly folded on her cheap cotton dress. From the distance came the high-pitched wail of an ambulance.

It ended quickly, with the ambulance driving away and the crowd thinning out. Rennon walked over to where the girl stood, looking sadly after the ambulance.

"May I have your name and address?" he said.

She turned frightened eyes on him. They were large, and deeply brown. Her hair was brown. Her nose had a most amusing tilt. She wore no make-up, and Rennon told himself confidently that on her it looked good.

"I don't suppose it would do any good to say I'm sorry," she said.

He showed her the page of names in his notebook. "Witnesses," he said.

"But I didn't see..." She smiled, and gave him her name. He printed it carefully. Miss Sharon Wheeler, Nurses' Annex, Brinston Memorial Hospital. He thanked her, and walked away slowly. He was half a block down the street before he realized that he was going in the wrong direction. He'd forgotten where he'd left his car.

Thadbury Z. Wheeler, Chief of Detectives, usually worked with his office door open. It did not take an appointment to see Thadbury Wheeler. All it required was nerve.

Rennon walked in quietly, picked up a chair, and set it down by Wheeler's desk. He arranged himself in it, and had a cigarette lit by the time Wheeler looked up.

Wheeler's scowl ran in widening ripples up the high arch of his bald head. "What's on your mind?"

Rennon puffed deeply, and aimed the smoke in the general direction of a half-opened window. Wheeler did not like smoke—any kind of smoke. He considered smoking a filthy, degenerate habit. Smoking in his presence required a long reach, because there were no ash trays in his office. The only suitable receptacle was a polished chromium-plated cuspidor. Wheeler chewed tobacco.

"I don't know, "Rennon said.

Wheeler got up abruptly, walked over to the door, and banged it shut. He returned to his chair and leaned forward, his massive hands folded over the stack of papers on his desk. "Give," he said.

"Do you know a good-looking girl named Sharon Wheeler?"

"Niece," Wheeler said,

"She doesn't look like you."

"That's a break for her. What's on your mind?"

Rennon grinned, and spoke carefully. "Being this day twenty-seven years of age, and of sound mind..." He looked up. "Am I of sound mind?"

"Lacking admissible evidence to the contrary..."

"Right," Rennon said. He leaned over and flicked his ashes into the cuspidor. "I've just been down to Traffic, going over some reports. Do you know how many pedestrians have recklessly flung themselves in front of cars in the last week?"

"Would it be inhumane of me to say I don't give a damn?"

"Do you know how many traffic accidents have occurred in the downtown area in the last week?"

Wheeler got out a plug of tobacco and took a man-sized bite. "Ditto," he said. "If memory serves me correctly, you were supposed to be looking for the Penman. Five thousand dollars worth of phony checks in the last six month. Did you expect to find him down in Traffic?"

"That last lead was not the Penman," Rennon said. "Some guy bought a five-dollar tie clasp and paid for it with a five-dollar check. The Penman does not write five-dollar checks. Anyway, he's probably in Los Angeles or Miami by now. He hasn't cashed a check for over a week."

Wheeler shrugged his busy eyebrows, and chewed rhythmically. "You didn't come in here just to read me a traffic report. What is it?"

"Being this day twenty-seven years of age, of sound mind, and of reasonable intelligence..." Rennon hesitated, got no response, and went on, "I was standing on the corner of Main and High Streets waiting for the light to change, and I found myself thinking the world was a pretty lousy place and I might as well end it all. I caught myself just as I was about to dive under a bus. And I heard someone laughing at me. I heard him in my mind. It was a most unpleasant laugh."

* * * *

Wheeler took aim, and rattled the cuspidor. "You've already used up this month's leave days."

"I backed away from the intersection to think things over," Rennon said, "And the next thing I knew, your niece slapped my face. She has an excellent slap. She said she heard someone say something insulting to her, and I was the first man she saw, so she slapped me. She also heard a laugh. I didn't cross-examine her, but my guess is that she heard it in her mind, just as I did. Our conversation was interrupted by a woman throwing herself in front of a car. She was killed."

"Is that all?"

"That's all. Except for the traffic reports. They're interesting."

Wheeler learned forward. "This is what I want you to do. Go back to the corner of Main and High Streets. This time, when you're about to dive under a bus, don't catch yourself."

Rennon got up. "Any objection to my looking into this in my spare time?"

"It's your time."

"Take a look at those traffic reports, will you?"

Wheeler gave him a long, questioning glance, and turned to his papers. "All right, I will."

Rennon moved the chair back against the wall and went out quickly, leaving the door open.

* * * *

"I can't be positive about it," Sharon Wheeler said. "My experience was different from yours, you see."

"It came to you as thoughts belonging to someone else. It came to me as my own thoughts. Yes, that is a difference." Rennon set down his empty coffee cup, and signaled the waitress. "Even so, something weird in going on. The traffic statistics prove that."

He sat admiring Sharon while the waitress refilled their coffee cups. She was in her nurse's uniform, looking crisply professional. The little restaurant was across the street from the hospital, and nurses and doctors seemed to be its principal patrons.

"What do you want to do?" Sharon asked.

"I have the names of some pedestrians who merely got hurt. Five of them are in your hospital. We might talk to them."

"We might. But it wouldn't do any harm to talk to Doctor Hilks, first. He's a resident psychiatrist, and he's sitting over there in the corner. Shall I call him over?"

The waitress delivered the message, and Doctor Hilks brought his coffee cup and joined them. He was a slender, middle-aged man with thick glasses and an awkwardly hidden bald spot. He nodded good-naturedly to Rennon, shook hands, and got himself settled on a wobbly chair.

He smiled indulgently when Rennon stated the problem, and he continued to smile as the facts were ticked off for him. He had his coffee cup refilled, he fussed impatiently with his watch fob, he polished his glasses, all the while eyeing Rennon with what the detective suspected was clinical curiosity.

"Hardly sufficient data to justify any kind of conclusion." he said when Rennon had finished. "The impulse to suicide is present to a degree in everyone. And I don't suppose it would be the first time that an attractive young lady has been insulted on Main Street."

"You aren't considering the upturn in traffic accidents," Rennon said.

"Any connection is purely speculative."

Rennon did not feel qualified to argue the point.

"Besides, you're postulating an impossibility. Telepathic communication is accepted by some scientists and vigorously denied by other. But even those who accept it don't claim that a telepath can transmit commands and insults—and laughs."

"What harm would it do to talk to the accident victims?'

"No harm," Doctor Hilks said. "But it won't be necessary. I've already talked to them. I've had several of them under hypnosis. I'm making a study of suicidal tendencies."

"You knew that?" Rennon said to Sharon.

"I knew Doctor Hilks had been seeing some of the accident victims."

"What did you find out?" he asked the doctor.

Hilks shrugged. "They all have suicidal tendencies. Look—have you got a card?"

Rennon passed on over, and Doctor Hilks scribbled on it and passed it back. Rennon read, "Doctor Homer Wallace, Lincoln Hotel."

"I'd suggest that you discuss your problem with Doctor Wallace, " Hilks said.

"Thank you," Rennon said. "I will."

* * * *

They went together to see Doctor Wallace, because doing things together came quite naturally to them. Rennon telephoned to ask for an appointment, and the doctor's dry, wispy voice informed him that Doctor Wallace was retired, had been retired for twenty years, and would treat no patients under any circumstances unless an accident of fate placed a cerebral hemorrhage in the corridor outside his door. Rennon told him the matter was personal, not medical, and the doctor gave in reluctantly.

The doctor occupied a two-room suite on the fifteenth floor. The sitting room was small, but as he tartly reminded them, quite adequate for one man. The doctor was small. Rennon estimated his height at five-feet-six, and thought that any healthy scales would consider his weight an insult. His face was grotesquely wrinkled; his few strands of hair were white. He was nearly ninety, and he looked his age.

Rennon described their experiences. The doctor pursed his lips, and allowed that it was interesting. Rennon mentioned the rising accident rate and Doctor Hills's interviews with surviving victims. "He suggested that we see you," he said.

"Why?" Doctor Wallace wanted to know.

* * * *

Rennon confessed that he did not know.

"I have discussed the matter with Hilks. He prates about suicidal tendencies. I consider him to be a fool."

"What is your explanation?" Rennon asked.

"There is no need to explain the obvious. We are dealing with thought transference on a unique level of effectiveness. Mental telepathy, if you like, removed from its normal status as unexplained and unproven phenomena. And you have reached the same conclusions, whether you realize it or not, or Hilks would not have sent you to me. He is having his little joke, you see, on all three of us, because he considers us candidates for his services. Well—let him have his joke, and his suicidal tendencies. Investigation will prove otherwise. But it is a matter for scientific investigation, young man, not police investigation."

"People are being killed," Rennon said. "That's a matter for police investigation. At least in my book."

"Nonsense. What would the police say if I were to inform them that there is a mad telepath loose in this city? They would hold me for observation. Telepathy has been a life-long hobby of mine. Many times in the past I have found what I considered to be obvious manifestations of telepathic communications. My colleagues have castigated and derided me. They have accused me of unprofessional conduct. One hospital at which I was a staff doctor threatened me with dismissal. Now I have proof, all the proof I or anyone else could need, and what can I do? I'm too old for crusading. Do what you like, young man, but your problem is no business of mine."

"One more week like this last one," Rennon said, "and we'll have more traffic fatalities than we had in all of last year. If you have any information that might help, it's your duty to step forward."

Doctor Wallace shook his head. "You can't catch a telepathic criminal. He could be anyone and he could be anywhere—a clerk in a store, someone walking along the street, a taxi driver, even one of your own policemen. If you did catch him, you could never prove he was the telepath. All he would have to do would be to stop transferring thoughts, and to all appearances he would be a perfectly normal citizen. If you could prove he was the telepath, you couldn't convict him. What law has he violated? There is no law against thinking, and there is no law against transference of thoughts to others. You'd better leave this to the scientists. The police won't be equipped to deal with a telepathic criminal until we have telepathic policemen."

"There must be something we can do. Will you come down and talk to my boss?"

"If he comes here, I'll talk to him," Doctor Wallace said. "A few more insults won't kill me."

Rennon arranged a meeting, and before it could take place it snowballed to include assorted police brass, two city councilmen, the mayor, and various business and civic leaders. Rennon had to arrange for a room to hold the crowd since Doctor Wallace's sitting room obviously wouldn't do. Then he had a twenty-minute argument on his hands to get Doctor Wallace to walk a few steps down the corridor and then turn left.

The conversation spiraled around slowly, and sometimes ranged from skepticism to derision. Rennon kept out of it. Doctor Wallace made it acidly clear that he did not expect to be believed, didn't particularly care if he wasn't, and didn't give a damn how many people were killed. He cited the experience of the surviving accident victims, several of whom claimed to have heard the same laugh Sergeant Rennon described. Would Sergeant Rennon testify as to his experience? Sergeant Rennon did so, and sat down.

"It is not surprising that so few of the victims recognize the presence of an outside agent," Doctor Wallace said. "The recipient of a projected thought accepts it as his own thought. It is only when the telepath has been sufficiently amused to laugh that the victim becomes aware of the alien mentality. At that moment it is usually too late."

Wheeler wanted to know if the doctor thought all the accidents were being caused by a telepath, and Doctor Wallace caustically reminded him that there had been accidents in the past without a telepath, and such accidents were probably continuing. The telepath should be blamed only for the number of accidents over and above normal experience. This, as the men from Traffic pointed out, was plenty.

* * * *

Traffic also pointed out that the idea of a telepath wasn't any more idiotic than some of the other explanations they'd been considering. Wheeler asked two questions, of nobody in particular. Is this idea to be accepted, and if so, what do we do about it? No one volunteered an answer to either question, and the conversation started spiraling all over again.

"Rennon," Wheeler snapped, "stop biting your fingernails and tell us what's on your mind."

"It seems to me, sir, "Rennon said, "that there are a number of steps which might help the situation. We can reduce the speed limit in the danger area to fifteen, and enforce it. We can make pedestrians stand back two feet from the curb when they are waiting to cross a street, and enforce that. We can spot first-aid stations around the downtown sector. Probably a number of stores would make space available. These things will make the public accident-conscious, and tend to prevent accidents—and get medical attention there fast when the accidents do happen."

"All that enforcement will take a lot of men, Wheeler said.

"Yes, sir. And as long as we have all those men in the business section, they can have a shot at looking for the telepath."

Heads nodded. If there was a way to send men out looking for a telepath without admitting that one existed, the majority clearly approved.

Doctor Wallace' voice sounded over the rumble of conversation. "Supposing you catch this telepath—and you will notice I'm waiving the questions of how you will know when you've caught him. Do you think locking him up would stop the accidents? He'll be able to project his thought from jail as well as from anywhere else."

"I'll worry about that after I catch him," Wheeler said.

One of the men from Traffic brought the meeting to a close. "Let's get moving. Some fool pedestrian may be diving under a car this minute."

* * * *

Rennon's ideas were put into effect but without his active assistance. Wheeler caught him just as he was about to be assigned to patrol a stretch of Second Avenue, and booted him out of the room. "Your job," Wheeler said, "is to catch me a telepath. Get going."

Rennon spent a morning in Traffic, meticulously marking the location of auto accidents and auto-pedestrian accidents on a large map of the downtown area. He tucked the map under his arm, and went over to the Lincoln Hotel to see Doctor Wallace.

The doctor was in a spry mood, perhaps as a result of the tentative acceptance by the city's leading citizens of the possibility of telepathy. He studied the map while Rennon talked.

"Brilliant," he said. "Absolutely brilliant. And absolutely impractical. You're assuming that the telepath reaches all his victims from the same spot, and that he is still there. Does that sound rational?"

"Perhaps not," Rennon said. "What I'd hoped was that I could pick out some favorite locations. And then—we have to assume that he stations himself where he can see his victims, and that may be a wild guess, but at least it's a beginning."

Doctor Wallace tapped the map. "The fatal weakness in your scheme is that no one knows the effective range of mental telepath. He may not be anywhere near his victims. He may be over in Bowerville," The doctor chuckled. "As far as that goes, he might be on Mars. Who can tell?"

Rennon folded his map wearily. "Mars is outside my jurisdiction. Whether we assume he's somewhere close by, or we give up. I have another idea. Since this started just over a week ago, I think it's possible that the telepath has just arrived here. I'm going to check hotel registers and rooming houses, to see who arrived about that time and is still here. And I might check those locations with my map."

"I have no faith in your map," the doctor said. "But I see nothing objectionable about the other approach. Whatever his station for projecting his thought, the telepath must sleep somewhere. And I note that the number of night accidents has not increased."

"That's right."

"Yes. That type of investigation might be fruitful. I wish you luck, young man." He sat with his head tilted back, his eyes half-closed. "It would be an experience, after all these years, to meet a genuine telepath. I'm almost tempted to go down and walk around the streets, to see if he would contact me as he did you."

* * * *

Rennon went downstairs and crossed the street to Groseman's Department Store. Groseman's had donated space to a first-aid station near its main entrance. An intern and two nurses were on duty. One of the nurses was Sharon Wheeler.

"We haven't had a call since we set up here," she said. "I think it's actually working."

"Maybe he's just holding off until he gets a line on what we're doing."

Rennon stood by the entrance, looking out at the passersby. 'It would be anyone of them," he thought. "Male or female."

An idea stabbed at him so suddenly that he reeled backwards. He sprang towards the first-aid station. "Second and High Streets," he said. "There's been an accident."

The intern grabbed for his bag.

"Wait a minute," Rennon said. He slumped into a chair and clutched at his head. "How did I know that? I wouldn't see that intersections from here."

The he heard the laugh.

Thadbury Wheeler charged into the store, and jerked Rennon to his feet. "Where the hell have you been?"

"Checking on accidents. There haven't been any."

"You didn't maybe stop to wonder *why* there haven't been any, did you? Too busy flirting with the nurses, I suppose."

"Uncle Thad?" Sharon exclaimed. "That's not fair. He's been..."

"I know what he's been doing. How do I know? The telepath slipped the word to me. Sergeant Rennon's over at Grosemen's aid station flirting with a nurse. That's why there haven't been any accidents. The telepath is too busy driving the force nuts to bother pedestrians. He slipped someone an idea that a shoe-store clerk is the telepath, and we wasted half an hour. Ten men dropped out of slight, and I found them all down at the depot. The telepath slipped the idea that he was departing on the two o'clock train. I say if he's departing, let him go. He even sent me chasing over to the Roosevelt Hotel. I was knocking on the door of room 517 before I realized what an ass I was making of myself. Fortunately no one was in. He's driving me crazy!"

"Even so," Rennon said, "it's better than people getting killed."

"He slips us something good now and then. Like an hour ago, when he put two of the boys onto a pickpocket. And like when he let me know my star detective was in here flirting with my niece. Sometimes he knocks off, too, and we don't hear from him for twenty, thirty minutes. But he comes back stronger than ever. Come along, now, and earn your pay."

They went out to the curb, where Wheeler's car stood. A patrol car came screaming around the corner, and roared away down Main Street. Wheeler said to his driver, "Find out where they're going."

The driver grabbed the radio. A block away, the patrol car slowed, and pulled over.

"They've decided they don't know," the driver said.

Wheeler said explosively, "Nuts!"

He climbed into the back seat, and Rennon got in beside him. Gloomily they listened to the radio, chaos of conflicting reports, false leads, and frantic dashes to non-existent accidents.

Suddenly Rennon started, and looked at Wheeler.

"Did you get that?" Wheeler said. "Four-car smash at Third and Elm?"

"I got it. I head the laugh, too."

"See if there's a car near there," Wheeler said to the driver. "We don't dare ignore it."

The driver got on the radio.

Wheeler straightened up again. "Rooming house at 11921 South River, Room Five."

The driver nodded.

"Roosevelt Hotel," Rennon said. "Room 517."

"Skip that," Wheeler snapped. "I've been there."

They stared at each other.

* * * *

"All right," Wheeler said. "Send it out. Maybe someone's home now."

Another patrol car went tearing past. Wheeler shrugged, and let it go. "I'm going to resign," he muttered. "I couldn't stand another day of this."

Rennon said nothing. The thought had reached him quite clearly that the telepath was hiding in the band shell at Riverside Park. He kept it to himself.

"We're licked," Wheeler muttered. "We wouldn't know him if we saw him. All he'd have to do would be keep his thoughts to himself. We might as well go back to headquarters."

The driver nodded, and turned the ignition key.

Suddenly Rennon leaped for the door. The thought he'd had was unlike all other thoughts, terrifying in its urgency. "Lincoln Hotel, 1548. Help! Please help!"

"Did you get that?" he called, but Wheeler was out on the other side, and starting across the street. Rennon dodged traffic and followed him. A patrol car swung to the curb as they reached the other side. Two uniformed officers came hurrying down the street. The siren of another patrol car sounded in the distance. Rennon looked back, and saw the intern and the two nurses come hurrying out of Groseman's. He ran after Wheeler, and caught him at the elevator.

Two detectives were there ahead of them. They smashed the door just as the hotel manager came into sight waving a key. Rennon bounded across the empty room, and opened a door. He was into the bedroom beyond before he realized where he was.

It was Doctor Wallace's suite.

The doctor lay on the floor. The small body seemed shriveled and insignificant, but the face was a mask of fierce triumph. Wheeler bent over him and shook his head.

Rennon turned to the window. A telescope stood on a tripod, pointing downwards. Rennon went back to the sitting room, sat down at the desk, and got out his map. He marked the location of the Lincoln Hotel, and began checking off the accident locations.

Wheeler bent over his shoulder. "Heart attack," he said. "Too much excitement."

"It figures," Rennon said.

"When the medical detachment clears out, we'll use that telescope. I'll give odds we can see ninety-five per cent of the places. This thing is so obvious we almost booted it. Only one telepathy expert in town, and him a dedicated fanatic. Probably he's been telling himself all his life that someday he'd show people. Probably he's been using that telescope for years, looking at the people down on the street, and thinking evil thoughts at them. And then one day last week—say, is this thing possible? It hardly seems so."

"He started showing them," Rennon said. "The wrong way."

Rennon handed Wheeler the map and led Sharon Wheeler out of the way while the body was being removed. "He seemed like a fine old man," she said. "A crank, maybe, but a crank with character. What do you think went wrong?"

"He had the wrong kind of character."

"Whatever he was," Wheeler said, "I'm glad this is over with."

Rennon, standing with his arm around Sharon Wheeler, felt a lurking, shivering uncertainty. It had happened before, and it would go on happening—pedestrians foolishly stepping into traffic, drivers doing idiotic things. And now, whenever it happened, he would be wondering.

"I guess Doctor Wallace has the last laugh," he said. "We'll never know for sure."

"Nuts," Wheeler said, "Of course it was Wallace. This will prove he's the one."

"The *only* one?" Rennon said.

Wheeler pushed the map aside and reached for a chaw of tobacco. For the first time in Rennon's memory, he had nothing to say.

AN ALIEN BY ANY OTHER NAME

The boy was small for his age. His trousers needed patching, his face washing, and his nose blowing. In the manner of small boys with these peculiarities, he picked up a stone and threw it. "A-Leon!" he screamed.

He missed, but the massive creature that was his target slowly, almost painfully raised itself a few inches above theground and shuffled away. With a full lifetime of bitter experience behind it, it knew when it wasn't wanted.

The first impression it made was that of a discarded carpet—a huge discarded carpet. It seemed enfolded in layerafter layer of flabby skin. The skin was covered with very fine, colorless hair, so scant that the creature looked bald. Its legs—no two people agreed about its legs. Some counted nine; others, insisting that there had to be an even number, made it twelve. Its face—did it actually have a face? There was a hump at the front center of the body that contained nostrils and what may have been a row of eyes. If it had anything so plebeian as a tail, this was concealed under one of the flaps of skin.

The explanation for its presence in Waukling Falls, Wisconsin, was simple enough but now almost forgotten. Old Bryan Lassinger, one of the first interstellar explorers, came from there, and, in the way of interstellar explorers, returned there when his days in space were over. He brought the A-Leon with him. No one knew what it was, or what its name was, or if it had a name. The tale Lassinger told was that the creature's mother had been killed in an unfortunate accident—Lassinger's ship had landed on it—and he himself had found foods the infant could eat, fed it, and cared for it. It became a pet, following him around like a dog, and there was no question of turning it loose to fend for itself when the humans left. It could not have survived.

He brought it back to Earth, and, eventually, to Waukling Falls, where it became everyone's pet. It was an alien from outer space, the first that the good people of Waukling Falls had seen, and the children loved it. They took to shouting, "Alien!" when they saw it. "Alien!" was soon corrupted to "A-Leon!" and that became its name.

Familiarity may not inevitably breed contempt, but it did in the A-Leon's case. Once it was no longer a novelty, people began to notice that it definitely was not a thing of beauty. As it became older, it continued to grow, and it filled Captain Lassinger's front yard—or a generously sized corner of the town square—when it stretched out to take a nap. It also ate a great deal. After the Captain's death, his daughter struggled for a time to keep the creature fed, but her meager income was simply not sufficient.

By that time, the A-Leon was an institution. Tourists came to look at it; local businessmen considered it an asset—one of the few Waukling Falls had. The town council voted an annual appropriation for the A-Leon's care and feeding, and private citizens supplemented this with donations of money and food. The creature may have been ugly, but it was the town's trade mark, and no one else had one. They hired an artist to paint its picture onto the signs that the Chamber of Commerce placed at the edge of town, and the local printer contrived a cut of the same picture so that anyone who wanted to could have it printed on stationery.

It was not until the next generation that tolerance turned to contempt. Young boys threw stones; young blades took to driving as close to the A-Leon as possible as they wheeled through the town square to give their dates a thrill. Its only place of refuge was the humble home of Granny Faulk, who remembered playing with the A-Leon as a child. When the town council cut the creature's food allowance, she squeezed her own meager income and planted a larger garden so the A-Leon wouldn't have to go hungry. Her home was always filled with children—her own grandchildren and all the neighboring children—and they were sternly taught to treat the A-Leon with gentle respect. Granny herself always had a moment to scratch it behind what she thought were its ears whenever it heaved itself into her path in a quest for attention.

On a warm summer afternoon, when she escorted her charges to Island Park, a small island in the Misquitosh River at the center of town, the children gleefully clomped onto the rickety, sagging wood bridge and stood at the half-way point, swaying as the bridge swayed, while they watched the A-Leon cavort in the water. It was a charming scene, but adults witnessing it were rarely appreciative. They were more likely to remark, with a frown, "We really ought to get that bridge fixed."

Granny Faulk peacefully sat in the park's tiny gazebo knitting warm winter stockings for her charges and chuckling at the A-Leon's antics. No one knew what sort of creature the A-Leon really was. It took to the water readily enough; on the other hand, it was awkward on land, but it always got where it wanted to go. Granny Faulk knew more about it than anyone else, and there was one thing she felt absolutely certain of—the A-Leon was no animal.

"In its own land, its people are cultured," she opined. "I've seen it on dark nights when there is no moon, singing as though to celebrate all the broken hearts in the universe.

Believe me, the A-Leon has real musical talent. A soft, moaning song, that's what it was, the lonliest song in the galaxy. And why not? There's no one within light years who can understand it, and no one on this entire planet to pay it any attention except snotty children and an oldster like me. Come around some dark night and listen, you'll hear a heart-breaking song such as you can't even imagine. I worry about what will happen to the A-Leon. Seems as though people treat it more unkindly every year."

Then came the year of rains. The rains started falling and kept right on falling and seemed likely to continue for the rest of the summer. Of course they did stop, eventually, as rains always do sooner or later, and the children—Granny Faulk's grandchildren and those of her neighbors—poked expectant noses out and reveled in the bright sunshine.

"Let's go look at the river," one of them suggested.

With a whoop, they were on their way—eight, ten, twelve, thirteen of them. nfortunately, none of them knew thirteen was an unlucky number. The old Misquitosh had risen far out of its bed. Island Park had shrunk to half its size, and the end of the bridge stood in six inches of water as the river overflowed its bank at that point.

The children were not deterred; they waded to the bridge and continued to whoop as they raced across the swaying structure. A gigantic splash sounded behind them as the A-Leon took to the water. The children screamed encouragement at it, and the ungainly creature hauled itself ashore on the island and collapsed, panting, while thirteen pairs of hands mauled it affectionately. Granny Faulk always said it knew when it was welcome, and the children in and around her home certainly made it welcome.

But after a few minutes of that, they turned to their own pursuits, exploring the newly formed shore line of the island while the A-Leon took to the water again.

Suddenly one of the children screamed an alarm. "The A-Leon—it's being washed away!"

The creature did indeed seem to be splashing frantically, and the rushing water was quickly sweeping it out of sight.

"What's that right behind it?" another child demanded.

There was a moment of silence. Then—"The bridge!"

They dashed to the other side of the island. The bridge was gone. They stood staring dumbfoundedly at the scar where the vanished bridge had stood. Over on the river bank, an adult noticed them, brought them to the attention of other adults, and in a short time a small crowd had gathered.

What the adults saw was a huddled group of frightened children on a shrinking island in a normally placid river that suddenly had become a raging torrent.

The adults shouted encouragement; the little group of frightened children remained frightened. Unfortunately, there was little that any of the adults could say or do to reassure them. "Where can we get a boat?" one of them asked.

The question was debated. A few men who fished on weekends had boats, but this time of year they kept them at one of the several lakes in the vicinity.

"It'd be hard to handle a boat in that water," someone observed. "The current seems to be getting swifter by the moment."

"Could someone swim over there?"

"Have to start way upstream and let the current carry you. If you did get ashore on the island, what then? How many of them are there?"

"Thirteen."

"In that current it'd take a pretty damned expert swimmer to rescue even one at a time."

"Maybe the A-Leon could help. Has anyone seen it? It's usually around here when the children come to play."

"Fifteen, twenty minutes ago I saw it in the river down by Matley's Mill. The current was so swift down there it couldn't get out, and it's almost as bad here. Not even the A-Leon could help the kids now, and the water is still rising. At that rate, all of Island Park will be covered in less than an hour."

A newcomer panted up, out-of-breath and in a panic. "Someone called from Larnfield. The dam has washed away. An hour from now, the river will be six or eight feet higher in Waukling Falls."

Someone whistled. "That'll cover the whole island and put the south edge of town under water, too. We'd better get moving."

"Hey! Don't forget the kids!"

"Ed, you stay here and keep an eye on them. We'll bring help." Most of the adults rushed away.

Several of the children had started to cry, which didn't make the waiting adults' ordeal any easier. Then more adults began to arrive. And more. The entire town of Waukling Falls was turning out.

And the circle of dry land where the children stood was getting smaller and smaller. Next to go was the gazebo, Granny Faulk's favorite place to sit. On the bank where the adults clustered, the gloom deepened. Then a car arrived with a boat trailer and a large rowboat. The gloom lifted at once.

"Ah! That's something like!"

It was not a proper place to launch a boat, however. They slide the boat off the trailer onto the river bank. Two men got into it with oars; everyone else pushed. The boat, the moment the current caught it, was swiftly pulled into the water and swept away.

"Should have started way upstream," someone grumbled. "Jim—take the car and trailer and follow them. Take a couple of men with you. If they can get to shore, tow the boat back here. Next time they can start far enough upstream to steer for the island."

Word quickly spread that a major tragedy was in the making. Two more boats arrived. The first was handled ineptly from the moment it touched the water. It swept past the island and vanished downstream. The men in the second miscalculated the currents, were swept against a tree in the now inundated part of the island, spun futilely as one whirlpool after another accepted them and then spat them out, and finally followed the fate of the first boat.

"My God!" a woman exclaimed. "Can't anyone do anything?"

"We're trying to get a helicopter, but there may not be one closer than Madison. There's a lot we could do if it was adults—get a rope over to them and haul them to shore, for one thing. But children are unpredictable. They'd let go at the wrong time, and the situation would instantly get worse. So—" He shrugged. "Here we are. We've already lost how many boats—three? And we don't know how many boatmen. The water keeps getting higher."

The island now was a bare bulge a mere fifteen feet in diameter, surrounded by a roaring river that seemed to have risen a foot every time it was looked at.

"What it amounts to," a woman said bitterly, "is this. We can't save the children, and if we keep trying, we're going to lose a lot of adults, too. I say—let's lose the adults. At least we will have tried."

"I haven't seen you parading in your swimming suit," a man told her angrily. "Let those who have to take the risk figure out what's to be done."

Several groups of men were trying to do just that. They were talking with deadly seriousness. One of them kept glancing up the street toward the highway. He had heard that another boat was on its way, this one with a motor. The latest theory was that a boat with a powerful motor could fight its way upstream—kept under control because of the motor—and beach at the downstream tip of what remained of the island. The children could be loaded in a few seconds; if there wasn't room for everyone and some adults had to be left behind, they could carry ropes with them in case the boat couldn't make it upstream a second time. There could be no doubt, now, that the torrent's full force was almost upon them.

"Great idea—on paper," one man muttered. "Paper boats don't sail very well." One of the marooned children was his grandson.

Suddenly there was a shout. A woman screamed. Something dark floated across the face of the sun, banked steeply, and skidded across the water to haul itself onto what was left of the island. Children's voices squealed, "A-Leon! A-Leon!"

"I'll be damned," a man grunted. "I've known that thing all my life, and I had no idea it could <u>fly</u>."

Another man shrugged. "So it got there, which is nice, but it pretty much leaves us where we were before except that we now have one A-Leon to rescue, too."

There seemed to be no answer to that. The A-Leon lay on the island's narrowing beach, panting, with children mauling and caressing it. Then, suddenly, it reared itself back, revealing a far greater multitude of legs than anyone had suspected. It seized one child and then another, and before the children could react, it took to the air.

It barely cleared the water as it headed toward the river bank. Adults scrambled to get out of its way, and it flew "like a water bug wiggles," one man remembered afterward. Rather than landing, it seemed to lower itself to the ground. There were plenty of adult arms waiting for the released children, but both of them paused to give the A-Leon a hug before they scampered away.

It lay motionless except for its massive, sobbing breaths. Finally, as though it were well aware that its greatest achievements were still ahead of it, it stirred, gained the air again, and flew to the island. This time it returned with three children—the three youngest and smallest. One of them, Ardelia Schofield, was tiny, blonde, and a natural-born cover girl, and it was she, along with Charlie Jance, reporter for the Waukling Falls Gazette, who transformed the rescue of the Waukling Falls children from a trite yarn about a tragedy that didn't happen into an interstellar drama. Charlie had arrived on the scene belatedly, blessing the fact that he always kept a camera in his car. Ardelia, when the A-Leon released her, turned just as Jance pointed his camera, threw her arms around some protruding part of alien anatomy that may have been the A-Leon's face, and kissed it. It was spontaneously done; it made a magnificent impromptu photo; and it was destined for calendar appearances all across the galaxy for centuries to come.

The A-Leon made a third trip, and a fourth. Each time its hulking body became airborne more laboriously. The fifth trip was the worst, and spectators feared that the A-Leon's magnificent heroics were about to terminate in a tragic anti-climax. The island had almost disappeared; the A-Leon barely cleared the water as it brought children numbers ten and eleven to safety. After massive, heaving sobs that seemed to contain the last of its life's breath, it headed for the island one final time. The last two children were the heaviest, and the A-Leon dragged folds of skin in the water as it flew. Several times it faltered and seemed about to plunge into the roaring river, but it kept the children dry and safe. Across the water's edge it soared, and then it folded into the ground in total collapse.

Jance, the newspaper reporter, had the presence of mind to gather all of the children around the A-Leon for photos. He actually managed to take several before he and the children were swept away by a late arriving Granny Faulk, who embraced as much of the A-Leon's unlikely anatomy as she could with her skinny arms.

"Good A-Leon!" she murmured. "You're a hero. All these cloddish humans stood around looking wise, and you did it. Leave it alone!" she snapped as Jance tried to arrange another photograph. "Can't you understand? It's a hero! It saved the lives of thirteen children, and it killed itself doing it!"

Suddenly the A-Leon began to moan, and those soft, wailing fluctuations of muted agony were the closest expression to pure music that anyone present had ever heard. The enormous, ungainly folds of skin heaved, heaved again, and were still.

The A-Leon had been loved by few people while it was still alive. It had to become a hero in order to make itself universally hated. First, immediately, came the question of what to do with it. A decaying carcass of those dimensions could well result in the necessity to evacuate the town. It would have to be buried, and quickly.

Burial immediately made people think of cemeteries. The children the A-Leon had rescued had attended various churches but any suggestion that the A-Leon be buried in one of their cemeteries brought talk of revolution and mayhem. Clearly the A-Leon had not been a Christian; probably it had never been baptized. All of the so-called "Christian" churches raised protests that Granny Faulk considered downright unchristian There would be no cemetery burial for the A-Leon.

"Phoey on all of you," she proclaimed. "That poor creature sacrificed its life to save the lives of thirteen children, and you deny it a place to rest its weary bones."

There was much shuffling of feet, but no one stepped forward to offer the large number of burial plots that would be necessary.

"Never mind," Granny Faulk said. "I wouldn't want it laid to rest among such unchristian people. It'll be buried right here on the river bank where it saved the children. That little hill would make a wonderful grave site. It overlooks the island, or it will when the river goes down again, and the A-Leon can lie there forever watching the children playing in the park."

That struck a poetic note, and the response was immediate. One of the men was all for getting his backhoe, digging the hole at once, towing the enormous body up the hill, and tipping it in.

"Oh, no you don't," Granny Faulk said. "First we have to get permission—doubtless someone owns this land. And then—it's not going to be a bare hole in the ground for our A-Leon. It deserves a nice mausoleum like the hero it is."

The justice of that couldn't be denied, though some doubted that it could be managed before the town would have to be evacuated. However, with such a powerful motivation, and with a group of eager people to work on it, much was accomplished quickly. Permission was obtained, a machine dug the hole, and masons from Waukling Falls and all the neighboring counties poured footings and quickly constructed a neat brick tomb for the A-Leon. Then—there was no other way—its body was dragged up the hill and toppled into it. This last was a rather inartistic touch, but no one could suggest anything better, and gas masks were already the "in" thing along the river bank.

A construction firm donated steel I-beams, and a cement slab was poured as a roof for the tomb. Fill dirt was added and landscaping performed, after which only a grave marker was required to complete the job.

Jed Pash, a farmer south of town, deftly solved the marker problem and at the same time solved a considerable problem for himself. There was an enormous granite boulder in his south pasture. It was of no Earthly use where it was; moved to the A-Leon's tomb, it would provide a wonderfully suitable grave marker for an alien of unknown origin.

* * * *

So it did. Moving it posed a considerable problem, but once placed on the little hill beside the river, it looked as though it had been there forever. Throughout the summer the landscaping touches continued. A gazebo similar to the island gazebo that had been washed away was constructed nearby. Flower beds bloomed lavishly along the walks that surrounded the tomb. When the water had finally gone down, a new bridge was built to the island, and someone put a new playground there. Granny Faulk enjoyed knitting in the new gazebo and watching children playing in their new park.

As the years passed, it gradually dawned on the townspeople that the A-Leon had embellished Waukling Falls's drab history with a priceless legend. Local businessmen noticed that an increasing number of tourists were stopping off to see the place of the A-Leon's miraculous rescue. The event was even described in tourist guides and indicated on maps as a tourist attraction—the only one Waukling Falls had. Because these tourists bought food, gas, and souvenirs, the A-Leon quickly became an important business. By subscription, enough money was raised to build a handsome little stone building near the tomb to serve as a museum. Charles Delsing, a young school teacher, became curator as a summer job and made himself the local A-Leon authority. Copies of old newspaper stories and photographs were framed and displayed. Extensive files were developed. The curator had a modest budget, so he hired a local artist to sculpt A-Leon's image—not life-sized, the little museum would have had no room for that, but large enough to attract amateur photographers from all over the continent.

The more Delsing worked with the A-Leon material, the more curious he became. The galaxy was no longer the splash of little known stars and planets it had been when Bryan Lessenger took to space. Large numbers of worlds had been charted and explored, and yet—when Delsing turned all of the reference resources of the state library loose on the problem, it seemed that no known world possessed any creature similar to the A-Leon.

Delsing expanded his research—first the Library of Congress, and then that of the United Nations, whose librarian, a Mr. Sung Soryan, attacked the problem brilliantly. He it was who found the only known reference in the entire galaxy to an alien creature that might possibly have been related to the A-Leon.

An explorer on an obscure world called Luxid had witnessed a strange event. A creature he had never seen before—he hadn't even recognized it as a life form at first, it more closely resembled a small excavation—was peacefully grazing. Suddenly two Fornfler noticed it from afar.

The Fornfler were a speedy and vicious carnivore. One had even outrun explorers in a land jet when they tried to overtake it. They had kept their speedometer at 110 kilometers, but it still managed to make its escape. There was little the explorers could have done for the peaceful herbivore except kill the carnivores, and interference with local life processes was something they tried to avoid. They resigned themselves to watching a gristly tragedy.

The carnivores quickly overhauled the herbivore. Then, miraculously, the herbivore seemed to shift to another gear. Its sudden burst of speed almost made it airborne. It was as though urgent need had conferred on it the ability to evoke a miracle. It vanished into the distance leaving the speedy carnivores staring after it.

"Urgent need conferred on it the ability to evoke a miracle," Delsing murmured. Suddenly he knew what had happened that day in Waukling Falls when tragedy threatened the lives of thirteen children. A placid alien from outer space responded to urgent need and evoked a miracle.

The explorer's account took its place with other material in the tiny A-Leon Museum. Children continued to play in the island park. Their favorite game was a looping merry-go-round that took the riders a short distance out over shallow water, and the children loved to pretend the merry-go-round was A-Leon, rescuing them from the flood by miraculously going airborne.

For Waukling Falls's adults, however, the area gradually came to be regarded with suspicion. In fact, with superstitious suspicion. Finally, some of them came right out and called the place haunted. After all, it was, in a way, a burial ground, and with alien creatures, one never knew. They described strange, chilling sights and sounds to be seen and heard there on dark nights. Adults tended to avoid the place, even in daylight.

The children pooh-pooed that. They had a legend of their own about the A-Leon, but they kept it to themselves. That legend said that if two or three of them chanced to play late on the island so that the first touches of darkness caught them just as they were leaving, maybe—just maybe—a huge, ungainly shape would come gliding in for an awkward landing in the shallow water at the north end of the island. If one of them were able to run back and tweak the

A-Leon's ears, or what seemed to be ears, before hurrying along home, the A-Leon would—

But that was the big part of a secret—the important part. What would the A-Leon do? Eddie Schwartz, whose lameness had miraculously disappeared, baffling his doctors—Eddie thought that he knew. And Marjorie Callan, the little blind girl who got her sight back—she thought she knew. And Sammy Adams, and Rachel Webber, and Alice Barnes—in fact, a number of children who had experienced miracles of greater or lesser impact—they thought they knew.

Up in the tiny A-Leon museum, that once-scholarly young man, Charles Delsing, who now was a dignified, bearded retiree and who had made the job of curator his life-long hobby, had been unable to learn anything at all about the children's silly legend, but as any of Waukling Falls's children could have pointed out to him, the really important things in life were much too complicated for adults to understand.

CPSIA information can be obtained
at www.ICGtesting.com
Printed in the USA
FFHW021700211119
56114185-62190FF